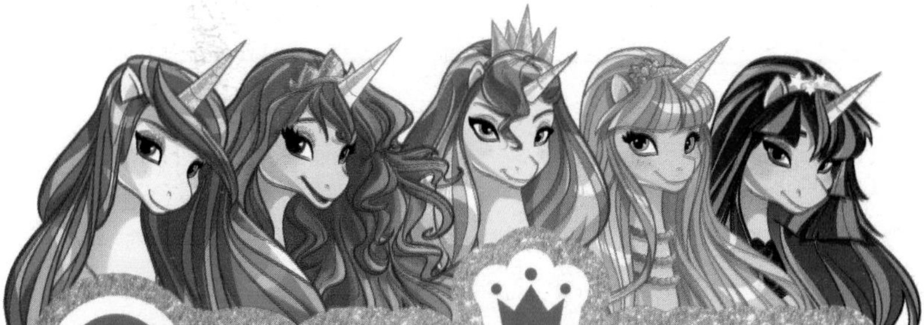

MELOWY

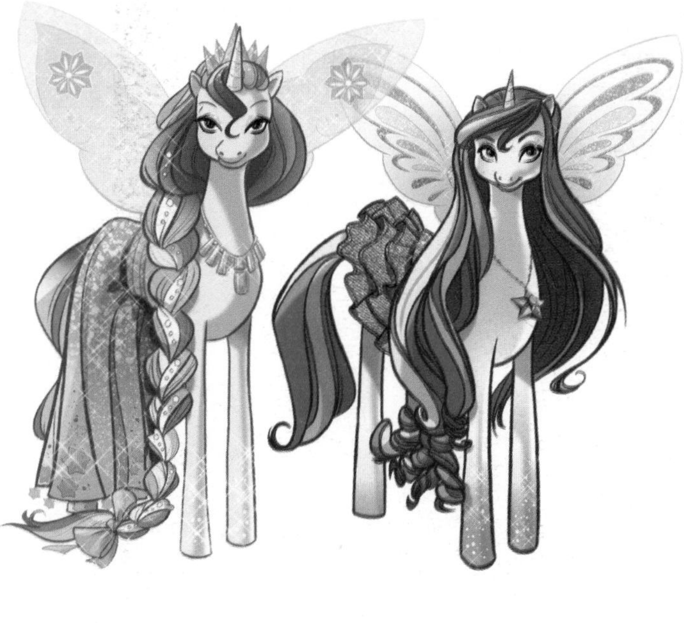

Josie
my book
this I like

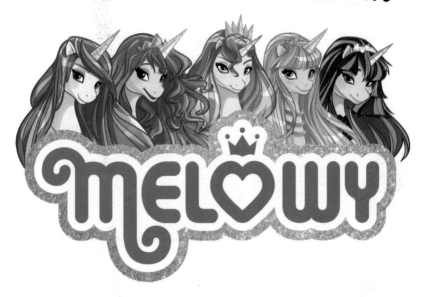

PAPERCUTZ™

MORE GREAT GRAPHIC NOVEL SERIES AVAILABLE FROM PAPERCUTᏃ

THE SMURFS 3 IN 1 #1

TROLLS 3 IN 1

THEA STILTON 3 IN 1 #1

GERONIMO STILTON 3 IN 1 #1

THE LOUD HOUSE 3 IN 1 #1

GEEKY F@B 5 #1

DINOSAUR EXPLORERS #1

SEA CREATURES #1

MANOSAURS #1

SCARLETT

ANNE OF GREEN BAGELS #1

DRACULA MARRIES FRANKENSTEIN!

THE RED SHOES

THE LITTLE MERMAID

FUZZY BASEBALL

HOTEL TRANSYLVANIA #1

BARBIE PUPPY PARTY #1

BARBIE STARLIGHT ADVENTURE #1

THE ONLY LIVING BOY #5

GUMBY #1

MELOWY #1

MELOWY #2

MELOWY #3

MONICA ADVENTURES #1

MONICA ADVENTURES #2

Go to papercutz.com for more!

Time to Fly

Script by **Cortney Powell**
Art by **Ryan Jampole**
MELOWY created by **Danielle Star**

PAPERCUTZ
New York

MELOWY #3
"Time to Fly"

Cover by RYAN JAMPOLE
Editorial supervision by ALESSANDRA BERELLO and LISA CAPIOTTO
(Atlantyca S.p.A.)
Script by CORTNEY POWELL
Art by RYAN JAMPOLE
Color by LAURIE E. SMITH
Lettering by WILSON RAMOS JR.

Production—JAYJAY JACKSON
Managing Editor—JEFF WHITMAN
Editorial Intern—KARR ANTUNES
JIM SALICRUP
Editor-in-Chief

Hardcover ISBN 978-1-5458-0309-7
Paperback ISBN 978-1-5458-0359-2

Printed in India
June 2019

Papercutz books may be purchased for business or promotional use.
For information on bulk purchases, please contact Macmillan
Corporate and Premium Sales Department at (800) 221-7945 x5442.

Distributed by Macmillan
First Printing

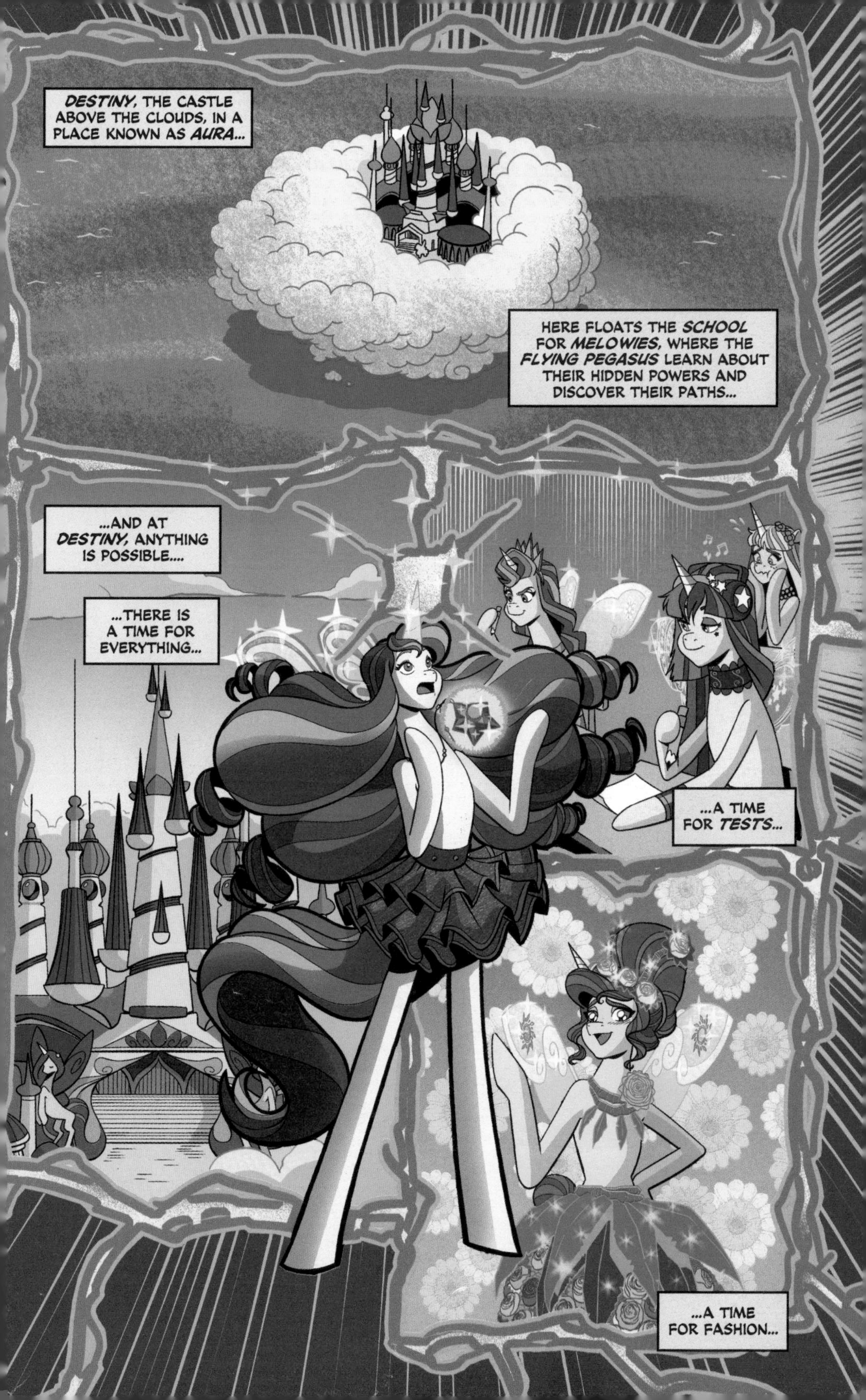
DESTINY, THE CASTLE ABOVE THE CLOUDS, IN A PLACE KNOWN AS AURA...
HERE FLOATS THE SCHOOL FOR MELOWIES, WHERE THE FLYING PEGASUS LEARN ABOUT THEIR HIDDEN POWERS AND DISCOVER THEIR PATHS...
...AND AT DESTINY, ANYTHING IS POSSIBLE....
...THERE IS A TIME FOR EVERYTHING...
...A TIME FOR TESTS...
...A TIME FOR FASHION...

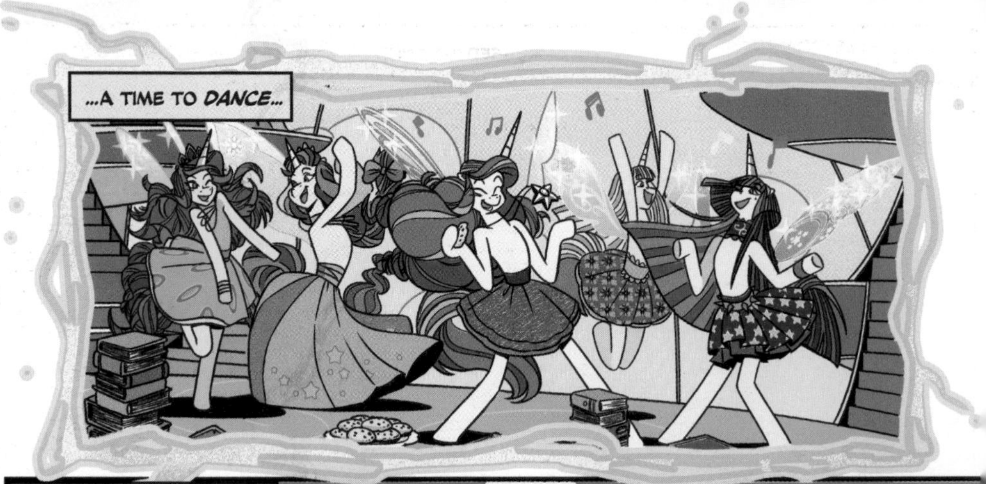
...A TIME TO DANCE...

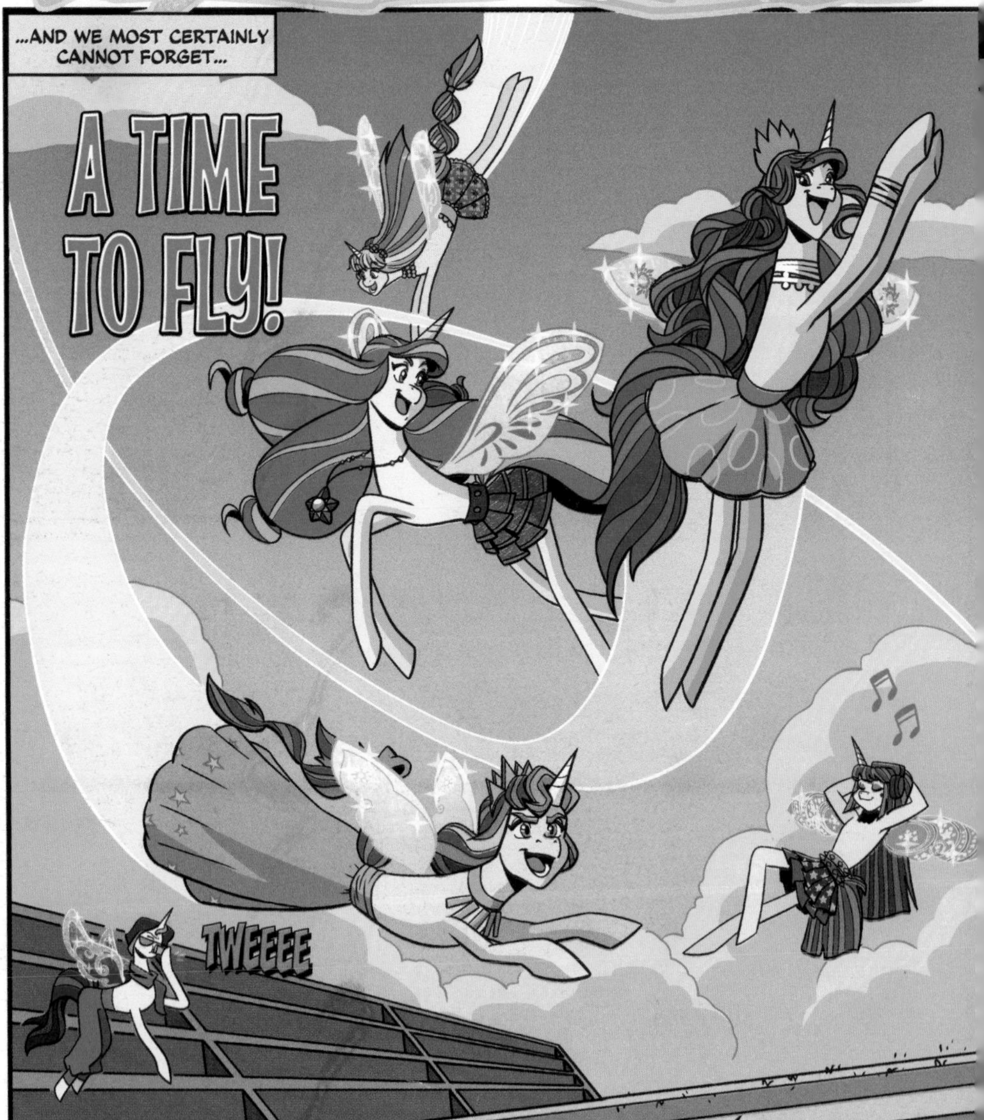
...AND WE MOST CERTAINLY CANNOT FORGET...
A TIME TO FLY!
TWEEEE

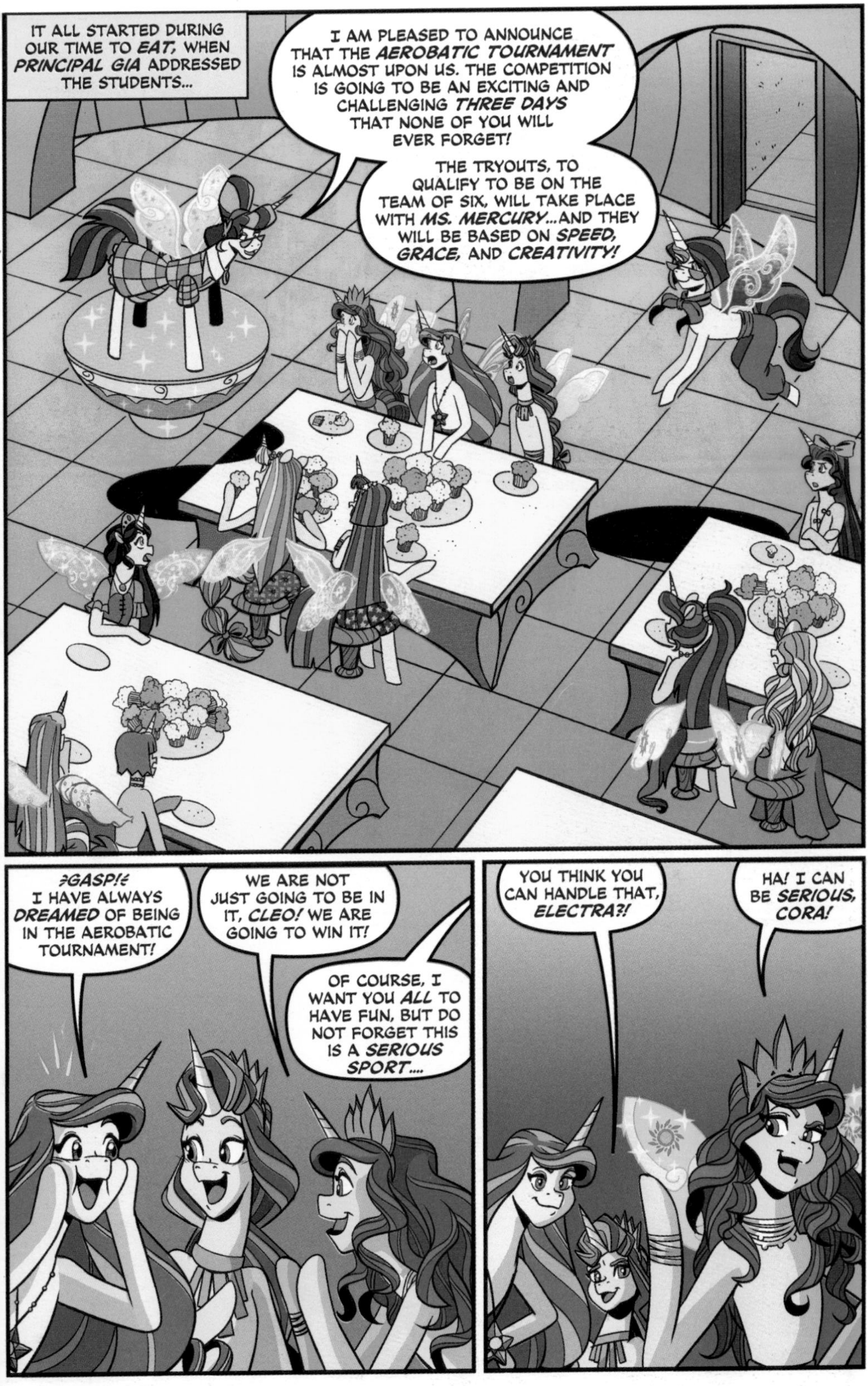
IT ALL STARTED DURING OUR TIME TO *EAT,* WHEN *PRINCIPAL GIA* ADDRESSED THE STUDENTS...
I AM PLEASED TO ANNOUNCE THAT THE *AEROBATIC TOURNAMENT* IS ALMOST UPON US. THE COMPETITION IS GOING TO BE AN EXCITING AND CHALLENGING *THREE DAYS* THAT NONE OF YOU WILL EVER FORGET!
THE TRYOUTS, TO QUALIFY TO BE ON THE TEAM OF SIX, WILL TAKE PLACE WITH *MS. MERCURY*...AND THEY WILL BE BASED ON *SPEED, GRACE,* AND *CREATIVITY!*
GASP! I HAVE ALWAYS *DREAMED* OF BEING IN THE AEROBATIC TOURNAMENT!
WE ARE NOT JUST GOING TO BE IN IT, *CLEO!* WE ARE GOING TO WIN IT!
OF COURSE, I WANT YOU *ALL* TO HAVE FUN, BUT DO NOT FORGET THIS IS A *SERIOUS SPORT*....
YOU THINK YOU CAN HANDLE THAT, *ELECTRA?!*
HA! I CAN BE *SERIOUS, CORA!*

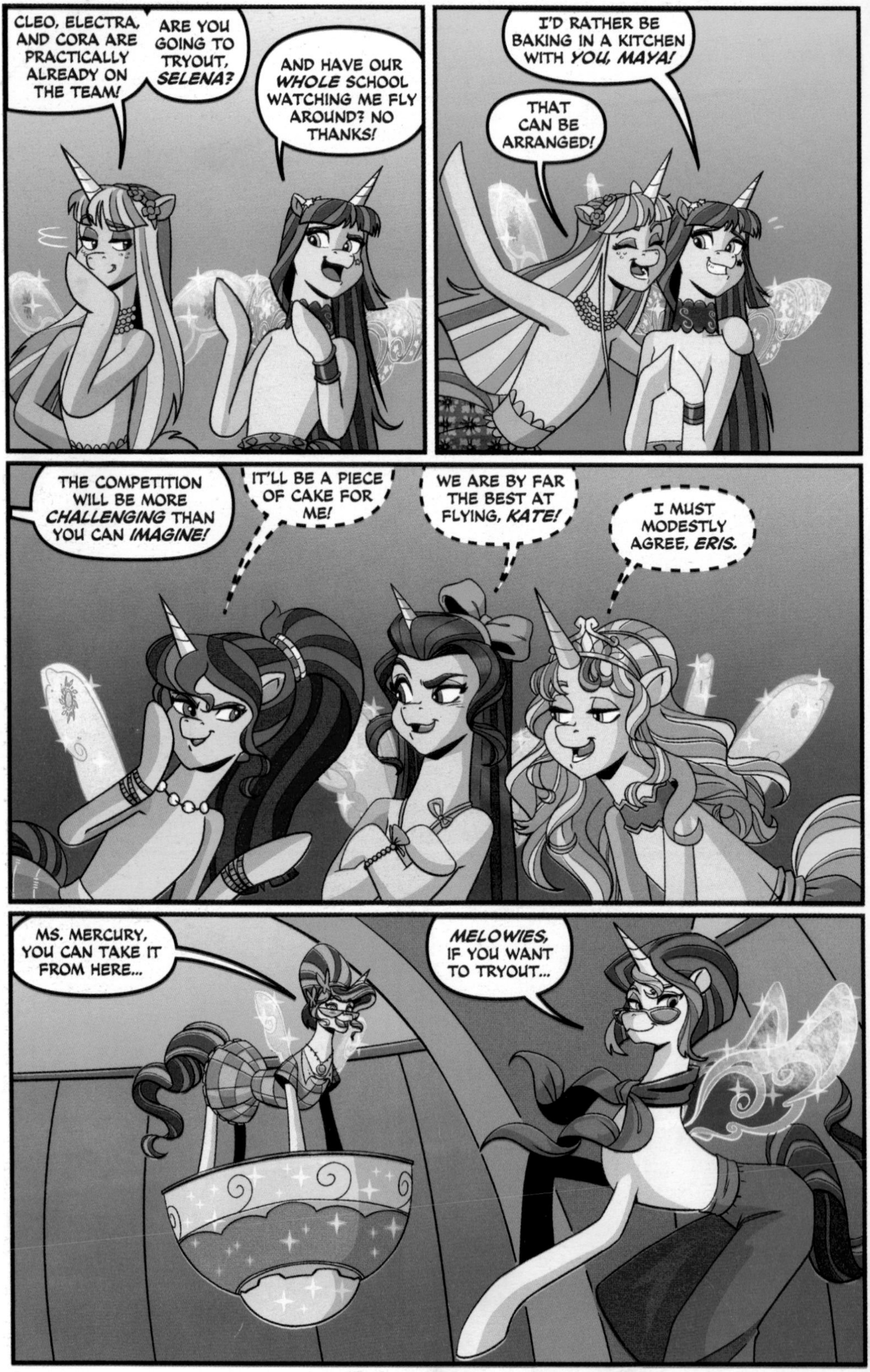
CLEO, ELECTRA, AND CORA ARE PRACTICALLY ALREADY ON THE TEAM!
ARE YOU GOING TO TRYOUT, SELENA?
AND HAVE OUR WHOLE SCHOOL WATCHING ME FLY AROUND? NO THANKS!
I'D RATHER BE BAKING IN A KITCHEN WITH YOU, MAYA!
THAT CAN BE ARRANGED!
THE COMPETITION WILL BE MORE CHALLENGING THAN YOU CAN IMAGINE!
IT'LL BE A PIECE OF CAKE FOR ME!
WE ARE BY FAR THE BEST AT FLYING, KATE!
I MUST MODESTLY AGREE, ERIS.
MS. MERCURY, YOU CAN TAKE IT FROM HERE...
MELOWIES, IF YOU WANT TO TRYOUT...

...FOLLOW ME!

WHAT ABOUT BREAKFAST?! IT'S THE MOST IMPORTANT MEAL OF THE DAY!

MAYA, JUST GRAB AND GO!

MOMENTS LATER...IN THE DESTINY SPORTS ARENA...

BETTER KEEP UP IF YOU WANT TO MAKE THE TEAM!

BE SURE TO FLY THROUGH EACH OF THE HOOPS, OR YOU'LL HAVE TO START OVER FROM THE BEGINNING!

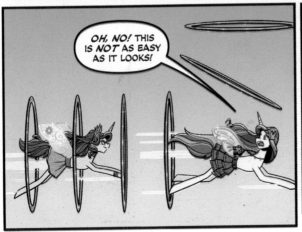

OH, NO! THIS IS NOT AS EASY AS IT LOOKS!

YOW! MS. MERCURY WASN'T KIDDING. THIS IS CHALLENGING!

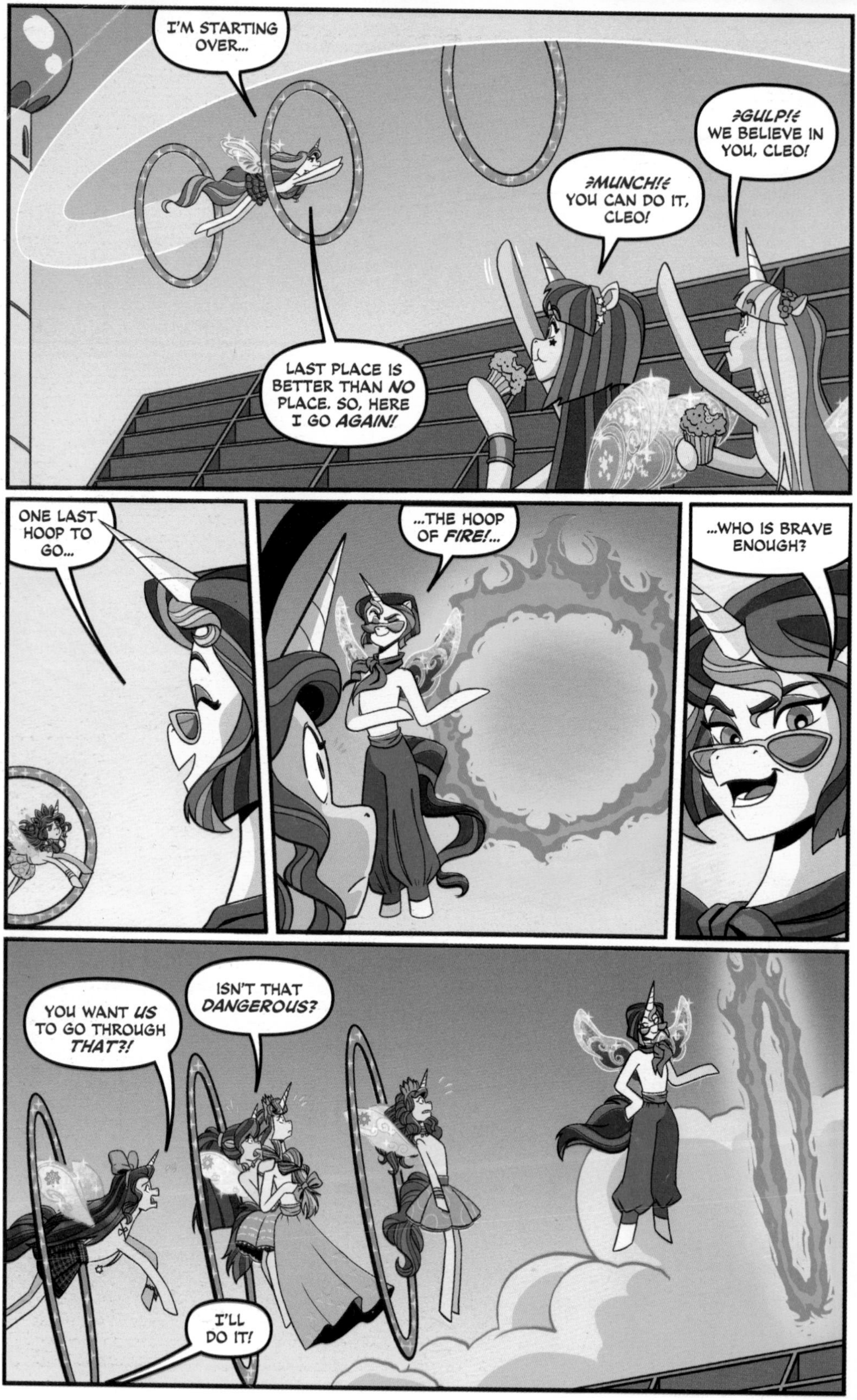
I'M STARTING OVER...
LAST PLACE IS BETTER THAN NO PLACE. SO, HERE I GO AGAIN!
MUNCH! YOU CAN DO IT, CLEO!
GULP! WE BELIEVE IN YOU, CLEO!
ONE LAST HOOP TO GO...
...THE HOOP OF FIRE!...
...WHO IS BRAVE ENOUGH?
YOU WANT US TO GO THROUGH THAT?!
ISN'T THAT DANGEROUS?
I'LL DO IT!

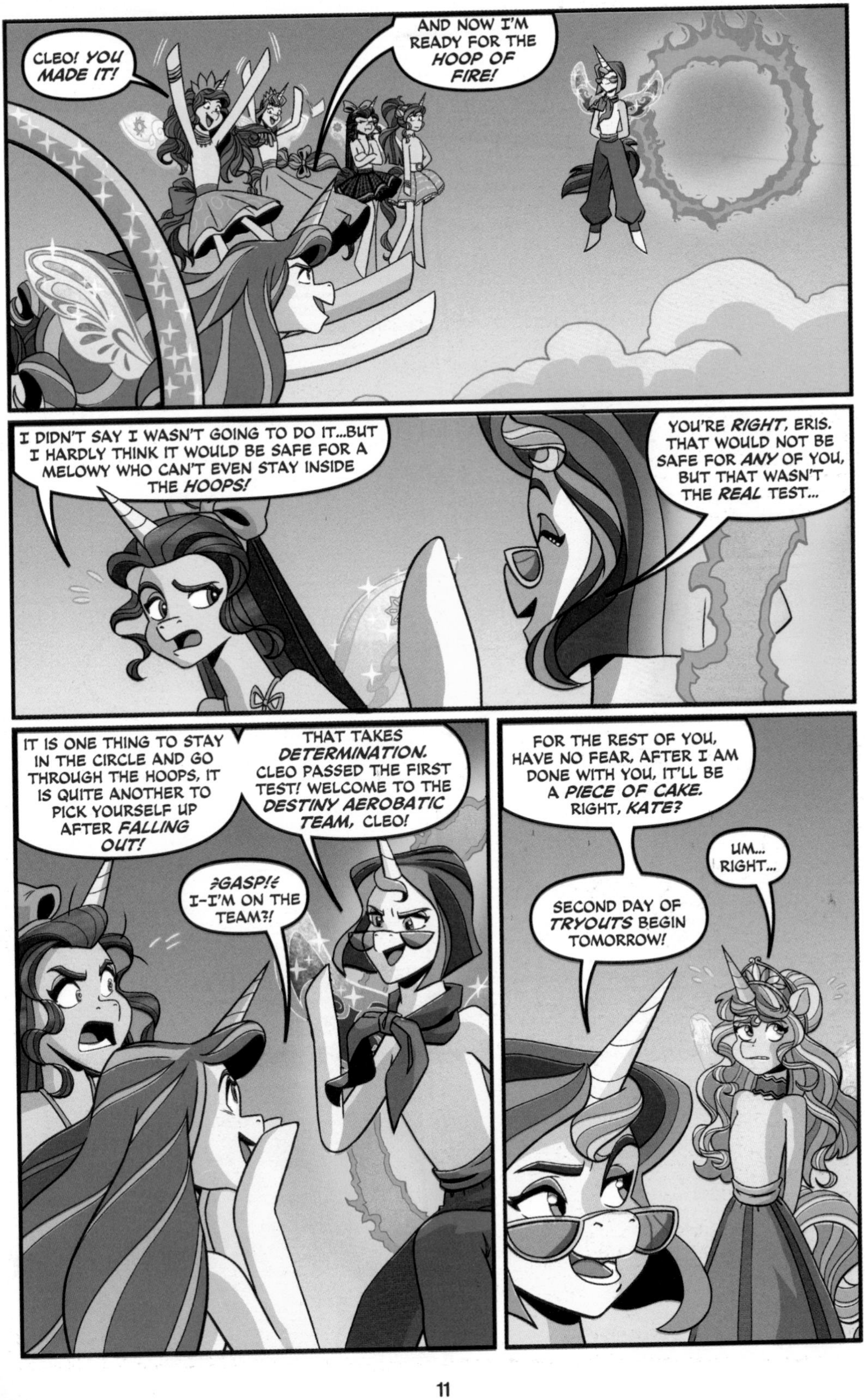
CLEO! YOU MADE IT!
AND NOW I'M READY FOR THE HOOP OF FIRE!
I DIDN'T SAY I WASN'T GOING TO DO IT...BUT I HARDLY THINK IT WOULD BE SAFE FOR A MELOWY WHO CAN'T EVEN STAY INSIDE THE HOOPS!
YOU'RE RIGHT, ERIS. THAT WOULD NOT BE SAFE FOR ANY OF YOU, BUT THAT WASN'T THE REAL TEST...
IT IS ONE THING TO STAY IN THE CIRCLE AND GO THROUGH THE HOOPS, IT IS QUITE ANOTHER TO PICK YOURSELF UP AFTER FALLING OUT!
THAT TAKES DETERMINATION. CLEO PASSED THE FIRST TEST! WELCOME TO THE DESTINY AEROBATIC TEAM, CLEO!
GASP! I-I'M ON THE TEAM?!
FOR THE REST OF YOU, HAVE NO FEAR, AFTER I AM DONE WITH YOU, IT'LL BE A PIECE OF CAKE. RIGHT, KATE?
UM... RIGHT...
SECOND DAY OF TRYOUTS BEGIN TOMORROW!

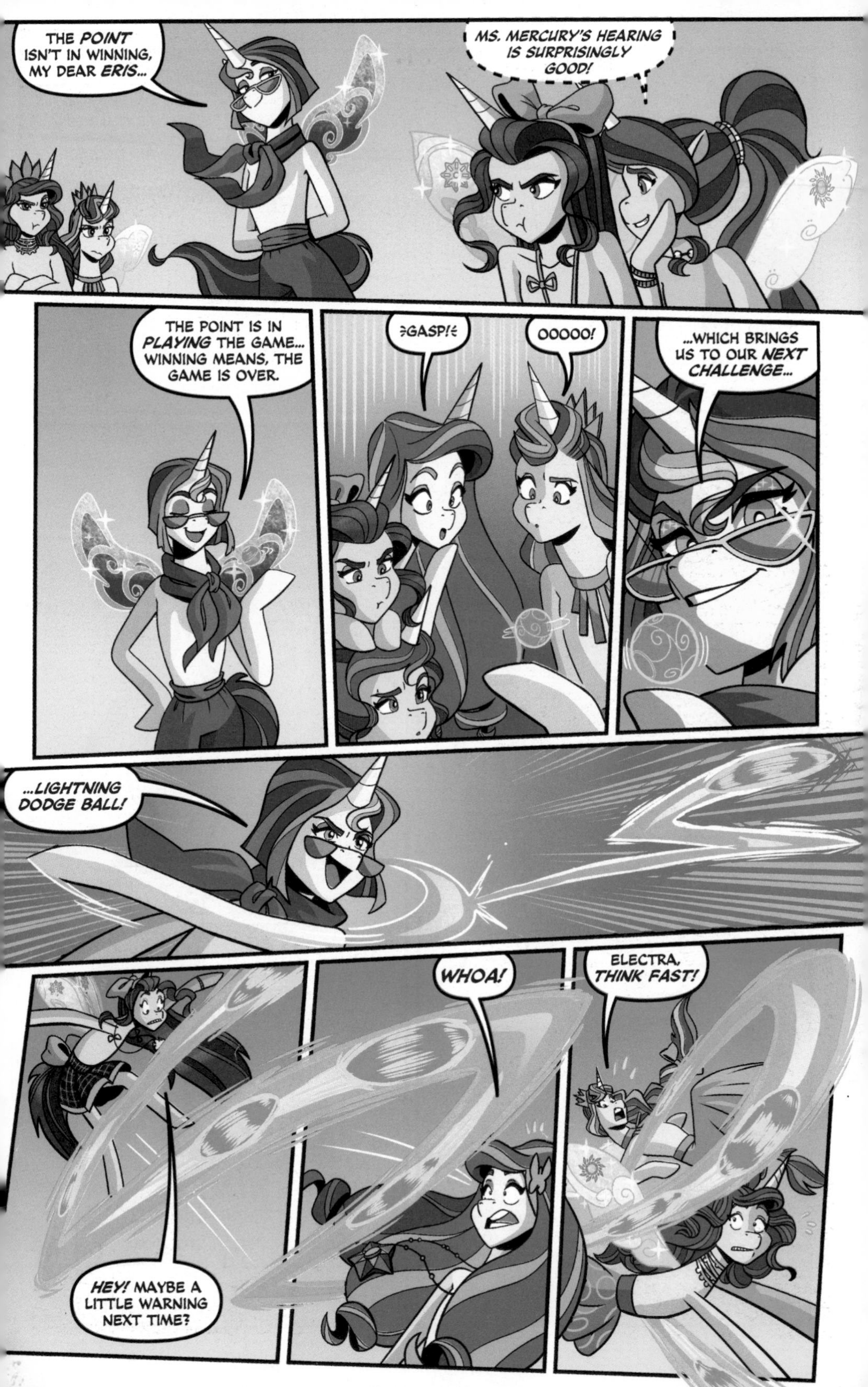
THE *POINT* ISN'T IN WINNING, MY DEAR *ERIS*...
MS. MERCURY'S HEARING IS SURPRISINGLY GOOD!
THE POINT IS IN *PLAYING* THE GAME... WINNING MEANS, THE GAME IS OVER.
GASP!
OOOOO!
...WHICH BRINGS US TO OUR *NEXT CHALLENGE*...
...LIGHTNING DODGE BALL!
WHOA!
HEY! MAYBE A LITTLE WARNING NEXT TIME?
ELECTRA, *THINK FAST!*

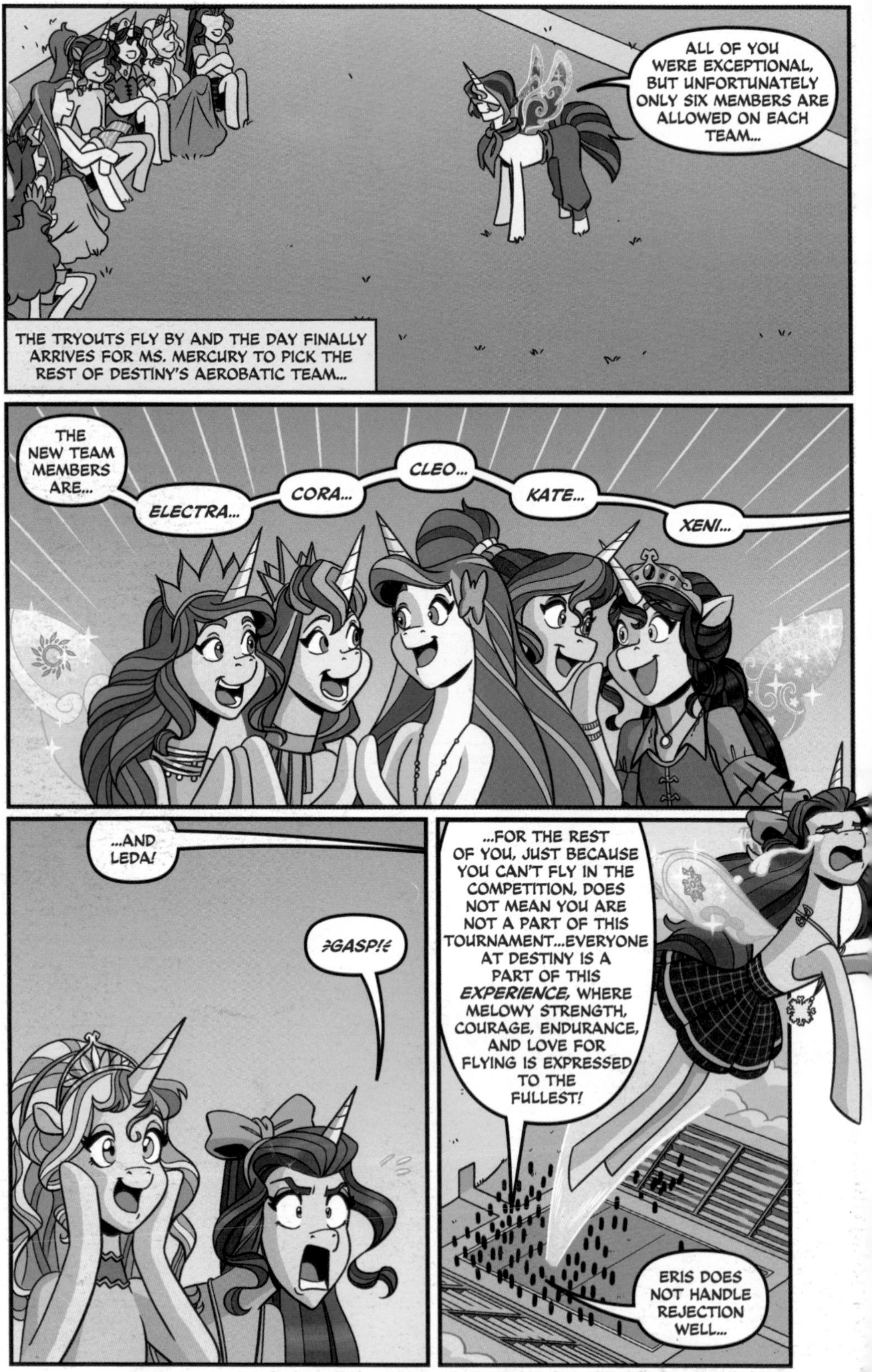
ALL OF YOU WERE EXCEPTIONAL, BUT UNFORTUNATELY ONLY SIX MEMBERS ARE ALLOWED ON EACH TEAM...
THE TRYOUTS FLY BY AND THE DAY FINALLY ARRIVES FOR MS. MERCURY TO PICK THE REST OF DESTINY'S AEROBATIC TEAM...
THE NEW TEAM MEMBERS ARE...
ELECTRA...
CORA...
CLEO...
KATE...
XENI...
...AND LEDA!
GASP!
...FOR THE REST OF YOU, JUST BECAUSE YOU CAN'T FLY IN THE COMPETITION, DOES NOT MEAN YOU ARE NOT A PART OF THIS TOURNAMENT...EVERYONE AT DESTINY IS A PART OF THIS *EXPERIENCE,* WHERE MELOWY STRENGTH, COURAGE, ENDURANCE, AND LOVE FOR FLYING IS EXPRESSED TO THE FULLEST!
ERIS DOES NOT HANDLE REJECTION WELL...

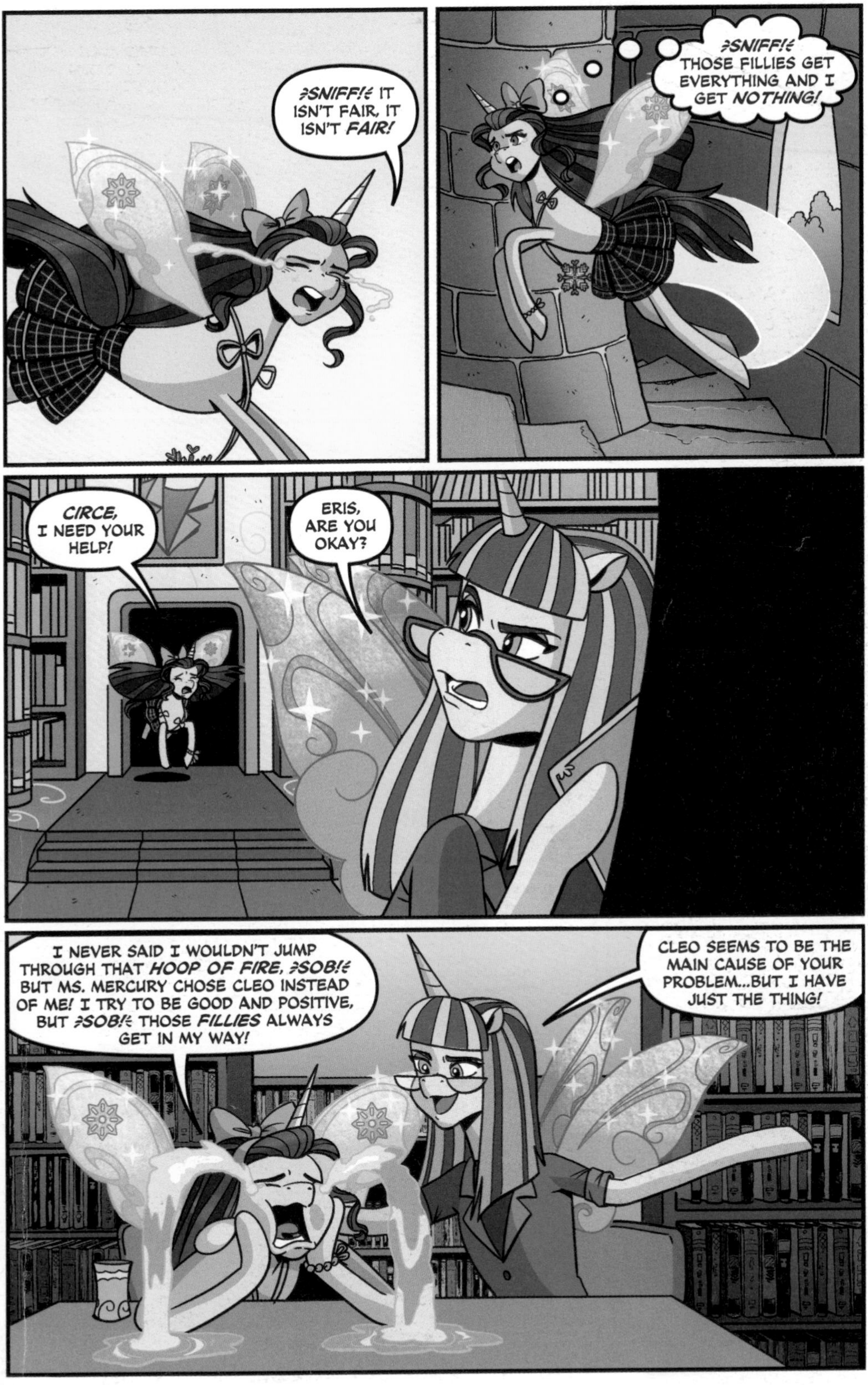
⸮SNIFF!⸮ IT ISN'T FAIR, IT ISN'T FAIR!
⸮SNIFF!⸮ THOSE FILLIES GET EVERYTHING AND I GET NOTHING!
CIRCE, I NEED YOUR HELP!
ERIS, ARE YOU OKAY?
I NEVER SAID I WOULDN'T JUMP THROUGH THAT HOOP OF FIRE, ⸮SOB!⸮ BUT MS. MERCURY CHOSE CLEO INSTEAD OF ME! I TRY TO BE GOOD AND POSITIVE, BUT ⸮SOB!⸮ THOSE FILLIES ALWAYS GET IN MY WAY!
CLEO SEEMS TO BE THE MAIN CAUSE OF YOUR PROBLEM...BUT I HAVE JUST THE THING!

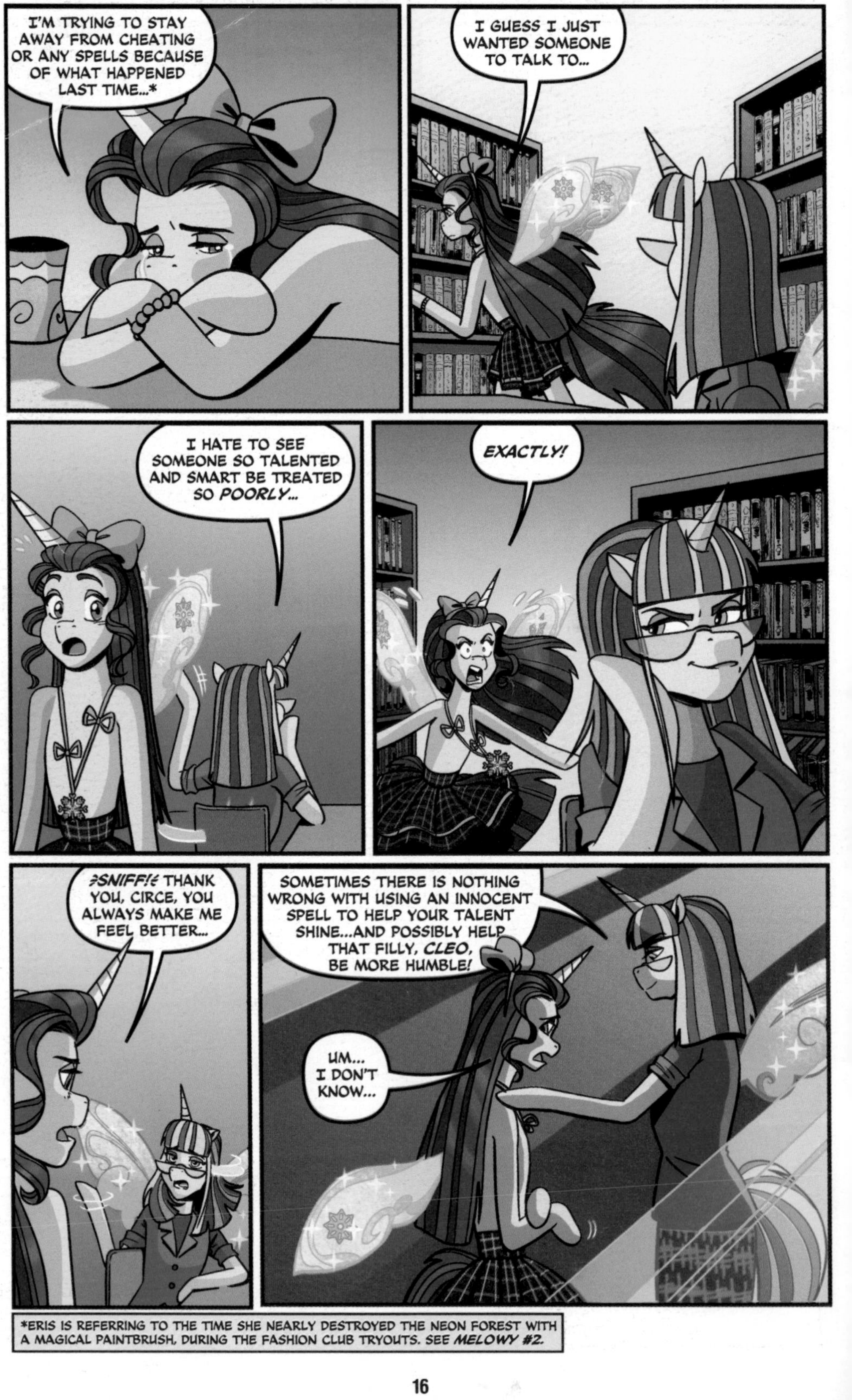
I'M TRYING TO STAY AWAY FROM CHEATING OR ANY SPELLS BECAUSE OF WHAT HAPPENED LAST TIME...*
I GUESS I JUST WANTED SOMEONE TO TALK TO...
I HATE TO SEE SOMEONE SO TALENTED AND SMART BE TREATED SO *POORLY*...
EXACTLY!
SNIFF! THANK YOU, CIRCE, YOU ALWAYS MAKE ME FEEL BETTER...
SOMETIMES THERE IS NOTHING WRONG WITH USING AN INNOCENT SPELL TO HELP YOUR TALENT SHINE...AND POSSIBLY HELP THAT FILLY, *CLEO*, BE MORE HUMBLE!
UM... I DON'T KNOW...

*ERIS IS REFERRING TO THE TIME SHE NEARLY DESTROYED THE NEON FOREST WITH A MAGICAL PAINTBRUSH, DURING THE FASHION CLUB TRYOUTS. SEE *MELOWY #2.*

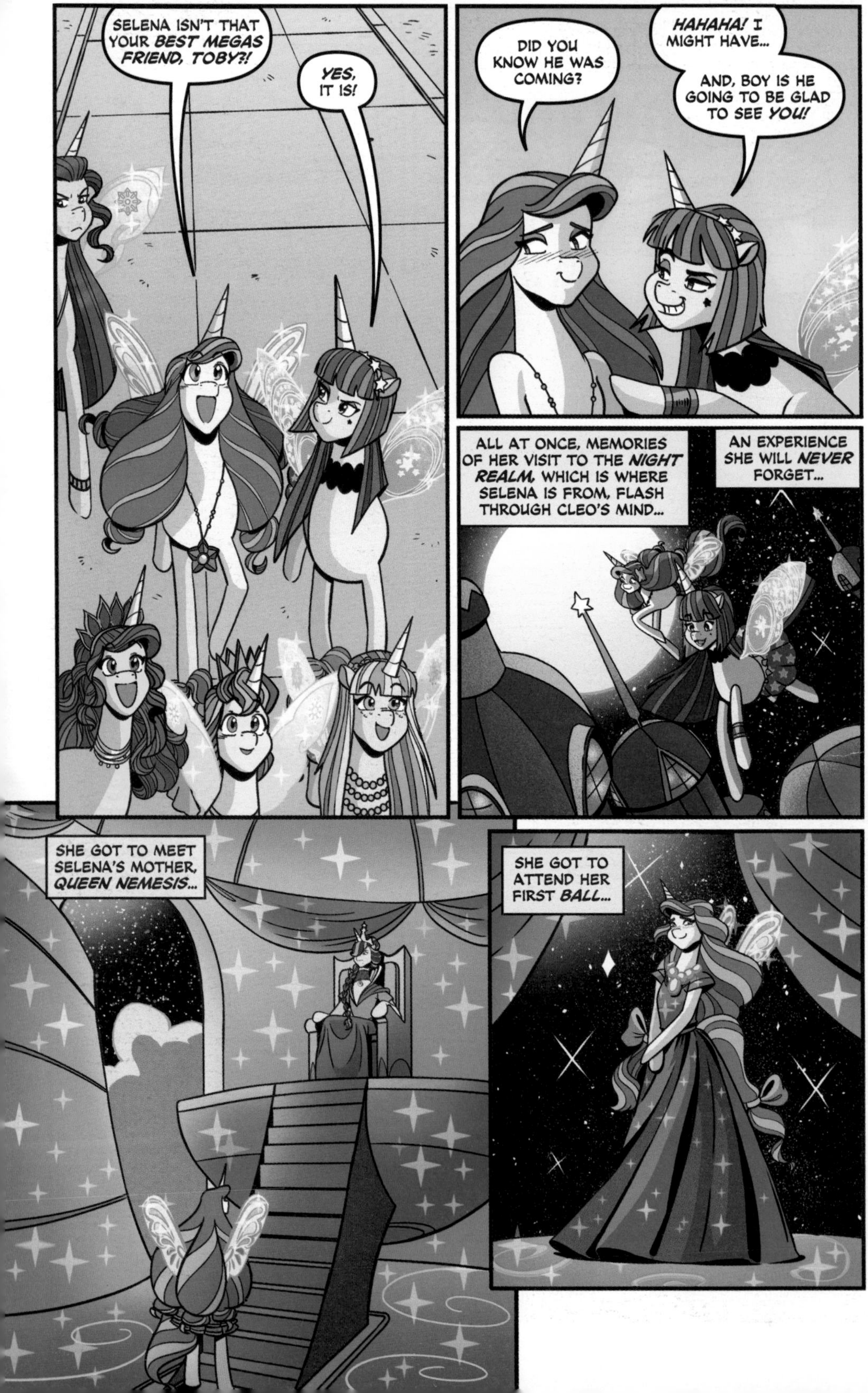
SELENA ISN'T THAT YOUR *BEST MEGAS FRIEND, TOBY?!*
YES, IT IS!
DID YOU KNOW HE WAS COMING?
HAHAHA! I MIGHT HAVE...
AND, BOY IS HE GOING TO BE GLAD TO SEE *YOU!*
ALL AT ONCE, MEMORIES OF HER VISIT TO THE *NIGHT REALM,* WHICH IS WHERE SELENA IS FROM, FLASH THROUGH CLEO'S MIND...
AN EXPERIENCE SHE WILL *NEVER* FORGET...
SHE GOT TO MEET SELENA'S MOTHER, *QUEEN NEMESIS...*
SHE GOT TO ATTEND HER FIRST *BALL...*

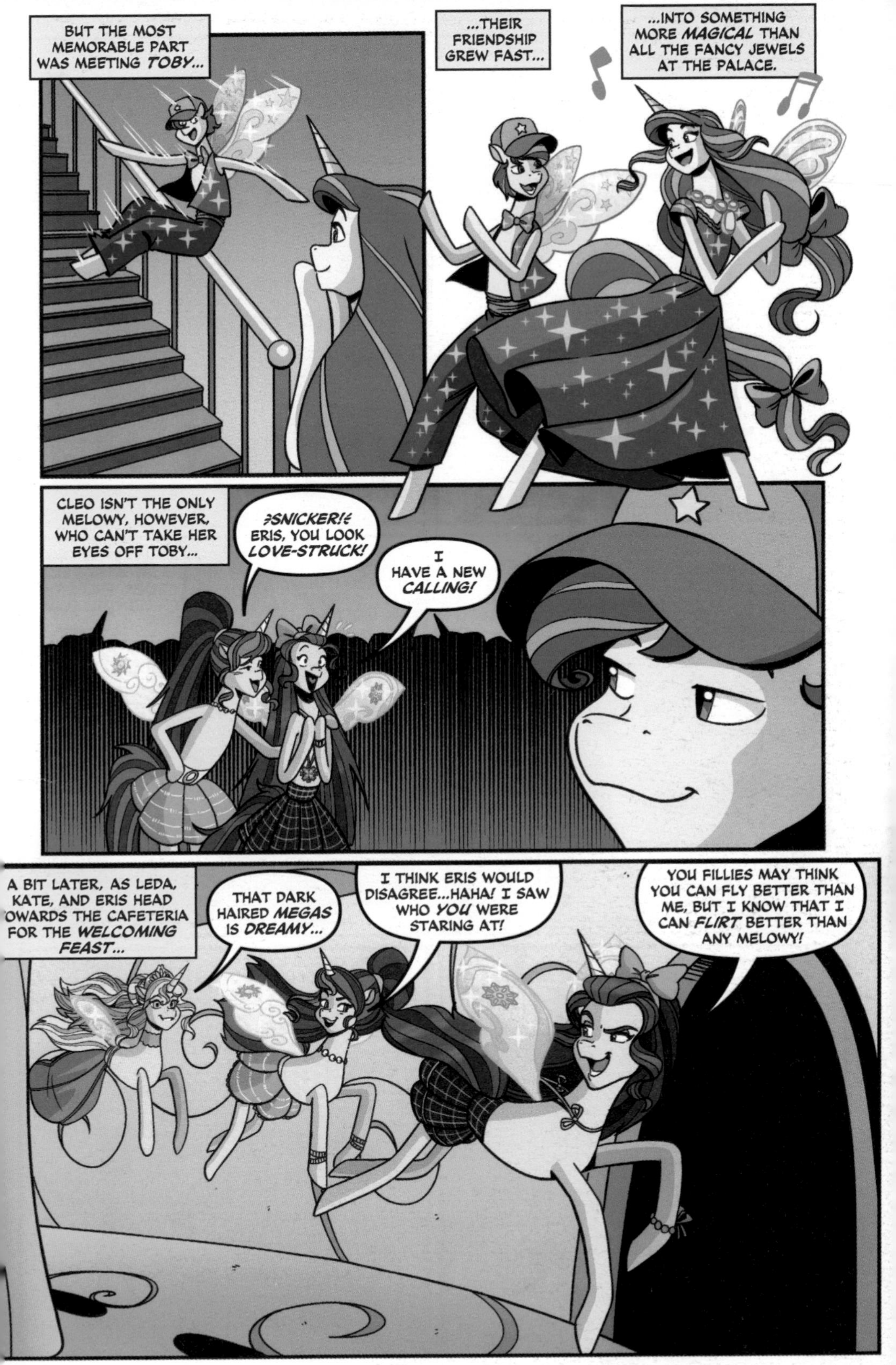
BUT THE MOST MEMORABLE PART WAS MEETING *TOBY*...
...THEIR FRIENDSHIP GREW FAST...
...INTO SOMETHING MORE *MAGICAL* THAN ALL THE FANCY JEWELS AT THE PALACE.
CLEO ISN'T THE ONLY MELOWY, HOWEVER, WHO CAN'T TAKE HER EYES OFF TOBY...
SNICKER! ERIS, YOU LOOK *LOVE-STRUCK!*
I HAVE A NEW *CALLING!*
A BIT LATER, AS LEDA, KATE, AND ERIS HEAD OWARDS THE CAFETERIA FOR THE *WELCOMING FEAST*...
THAT DARK HAIRED *MEGAS* IS *DREAMY*...
I THINK ERIS WOULD DISAGREE...HAHA! I SAW WHO *YOU* WERE STARING AT!
YOU FILLIES MAY THINK YOU CAN FLY BETTER THAN ME, BUT I KNOW THAT I CAN *FLIRT* BETTER THAN ANY MELOWY!

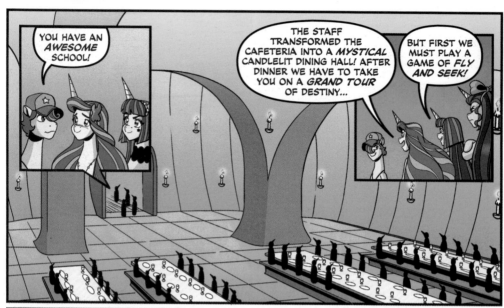

YOU HAVE AN *AWESOME* SCHOOL!

THE STAFF TRANSFORMED THE CAFETERIA INTO A *MYSTICAL* CANDLELIT DINING HALL! AFTER DINNER WE HAVE TO TAKE YOU ON A *GRAND TOUR* OF DESTINY...

BUT FIRST WE MUST PLAY A GAME OF *FLY AND SEEK!*

OW!

SORRY, THERE WAS A *WEED* FROM WHEN YOU RAN INTO THAT TREE AT PRACTICE...

HEY, I'M ERIS...YOU SHOULD SIT WITH ME AND I CAN TELL YOU ALL ABOUT HOW CLEO *TRICKED* MS. MERCURY INTO LETTING HER BE ON THE TEAM...

UM, ERIS, THIS IS MY BEST FRIEND, TOBY, FROM THE NIGHT REALM!

I'M SURE YOU MEANT TO SAY, YOU WANT TO TELL HOW CLEO, BECAUSE OF HER BRAVERY, WAS CHOSEN *FIRST* TO BE ON THE TEAM!

IT WAS A PLEASURE MEETING YOU, ERIS, BUT CAN I TAKE A RAIN CHECK, SO I CAN CATCH UP WITH MY FRIENDS?

OKAY, BUT IF YOU GET *BORED*, COME FIND ME!

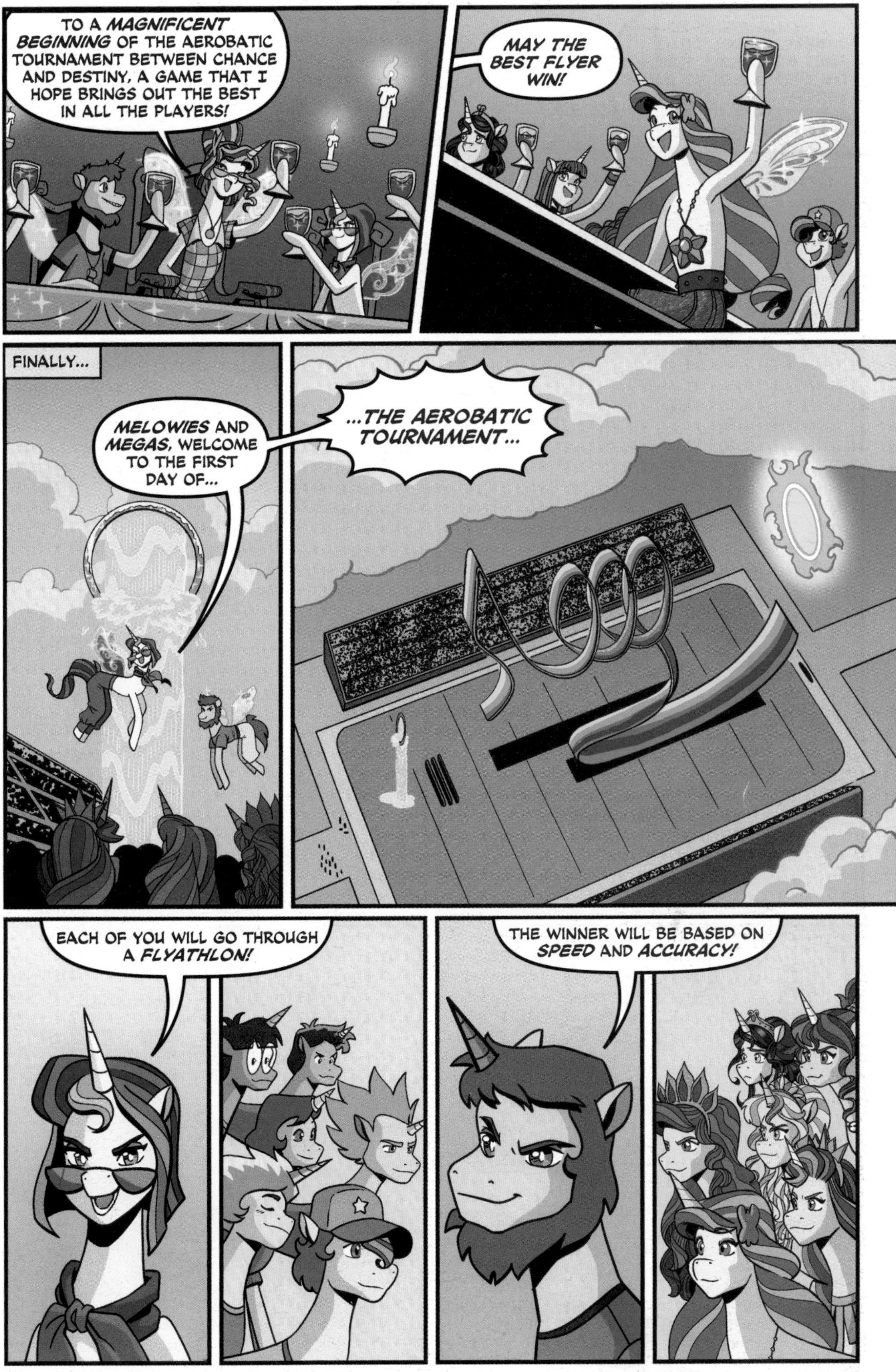
TO A MAGNIFICENT BEGINNING OF THE AEROBATIC TOURNAMENT BETWEEN CHANCE AND DESTINY, A GAME THAT I HOPE BRINGS OUT THE BEST IN ALL THE PLAYERS!
MAY THE BEST FLYER WIN!
FINALLY...
MELOWIES AND MEGAS, WELCOME TO THE FIRST DAY OF...
...THE AEROBATIC TOURNAMENT...
EACH OF YOU WILL GO THROUGH A FLYATHLON!
THE WINNER WILL BE BASED ON SPEED AND ACCURACY!

22

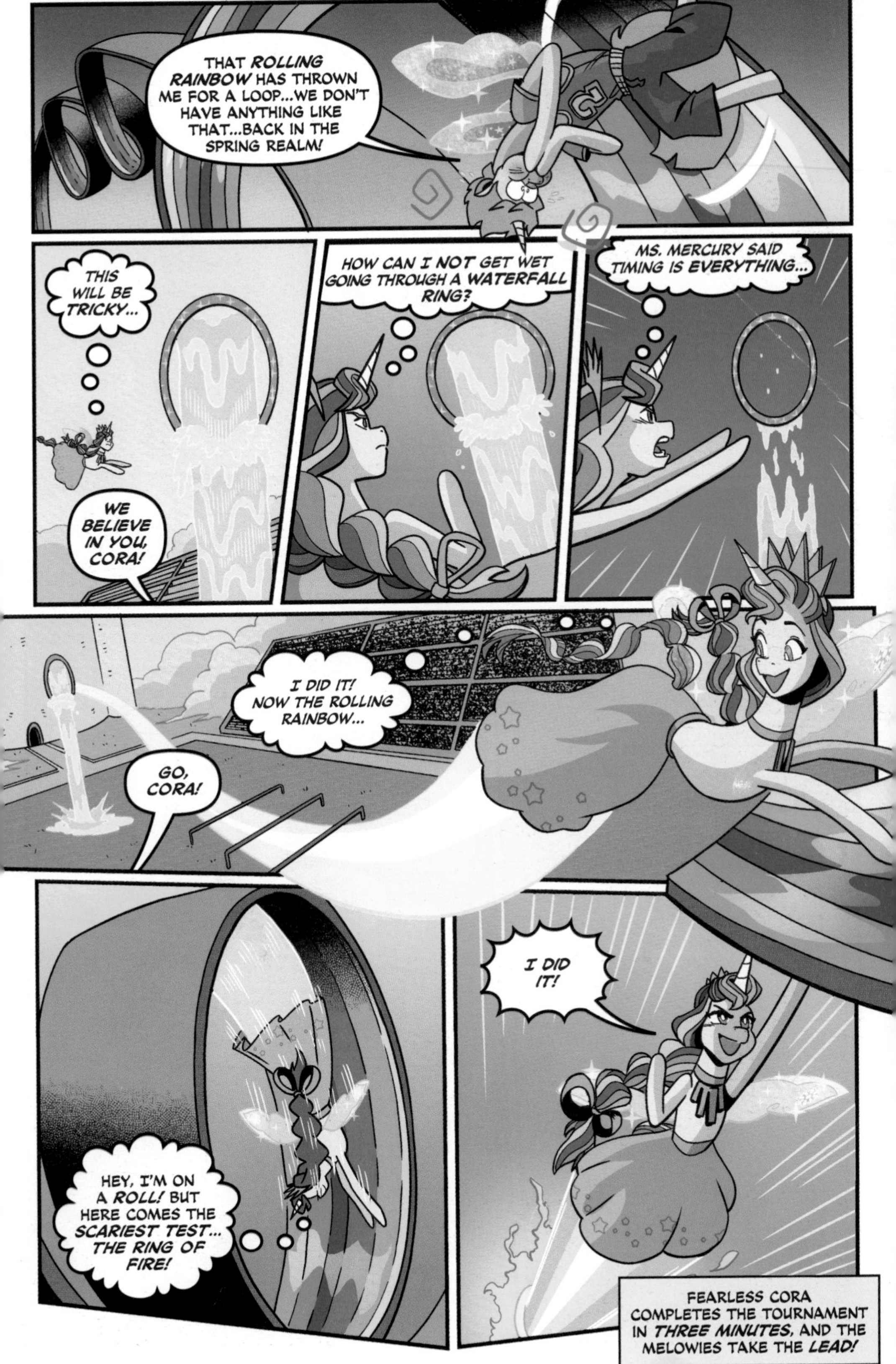
THAT ROLLING RAINBOW HAS THROWN ME FOR A LOOP...WE DON'T HAVE ANYTHING LIKE THAT...BACK IN THE SPRING REALM!
THIS WILL BE TRICKY...
WE BELIEVE IN YOU, CORA!
HOW CAN I NOT GET WET GOING THROUGH A WATERFALL RING?
MS. MERCURY SAID TIMING IS EVERYTHING...
I DID IT! NOW THE ROLLING RAINBOW...
GO, CORA!
HEY, I'M ON A ROLL! BUT HERE COMES THE SCARIEST TEST... THE RING OF FIRE!
I DID IT!
FEARLESS CORA COMPLETES THE TOURNAMENT IN THREE MINUTES, AND THE MELOWIES TAKE THE LEAD!

BUT NOT FOR LONG...AS A *DAY REALM* MEGAS SHOOTS THROUGH THE TOURNAMENT WITH BLAZING SPEED! *TWO POINT FIVE MINUTES!*

ϞWHEW!ϟ

YAY! DAY REALM! YAY!

MEANWHILE, SOMEWHERE OVER THE RAINBOW...

...THE COMPETITION IS REALLY *HEATING UP!* BUT I'M *ON FIRE!*

GO, ELECTRA!

FIGURATIVELY, THAT IS!

AND ELECTRA FIERCELY FLIES THROUGH THE FINISH LINE IN UNDER TWO MINUTES!

THE MELOWIES AND MEGAS ARE NOW *TIED!*

THIS IS IT, I'M THE LAST MEGAS UP!

MUST STAY *FOCUSED...*

GO, *TOBY!*

HE'S STILL *UNDER* A MINUTE!

SURF'S UP!

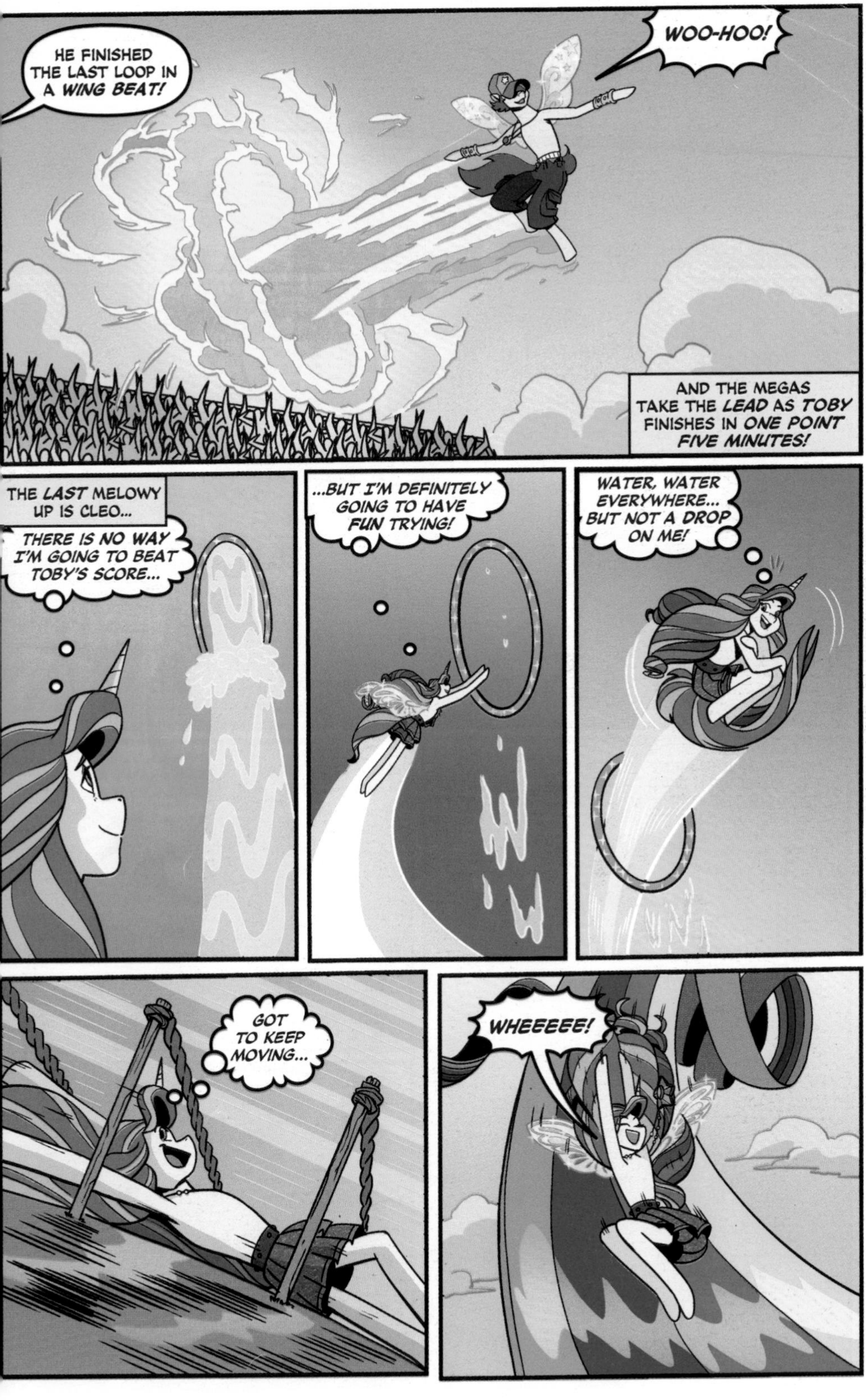

HE FINISHED THE LAST LOOP IN A WING BEAT!
WOO-HOO!
AND THE MEGAS TAKE THE LEAD AS TOBY FINISHES IN ONE POINT FIVE MINUTES!
THE LAST MELOWY UP IS CLEO...
THERE IS NO WAY I'M GOING TO BEAT TOBY'S SCORE...
...BUT I'M DEFINITELY GOING TO HAVE FUN TRYING!
WATER, WATER EVERYWHERE... BUT NOT A DROP ON ME!
GOT TO KEEP MOVING...
WHEEEEE!

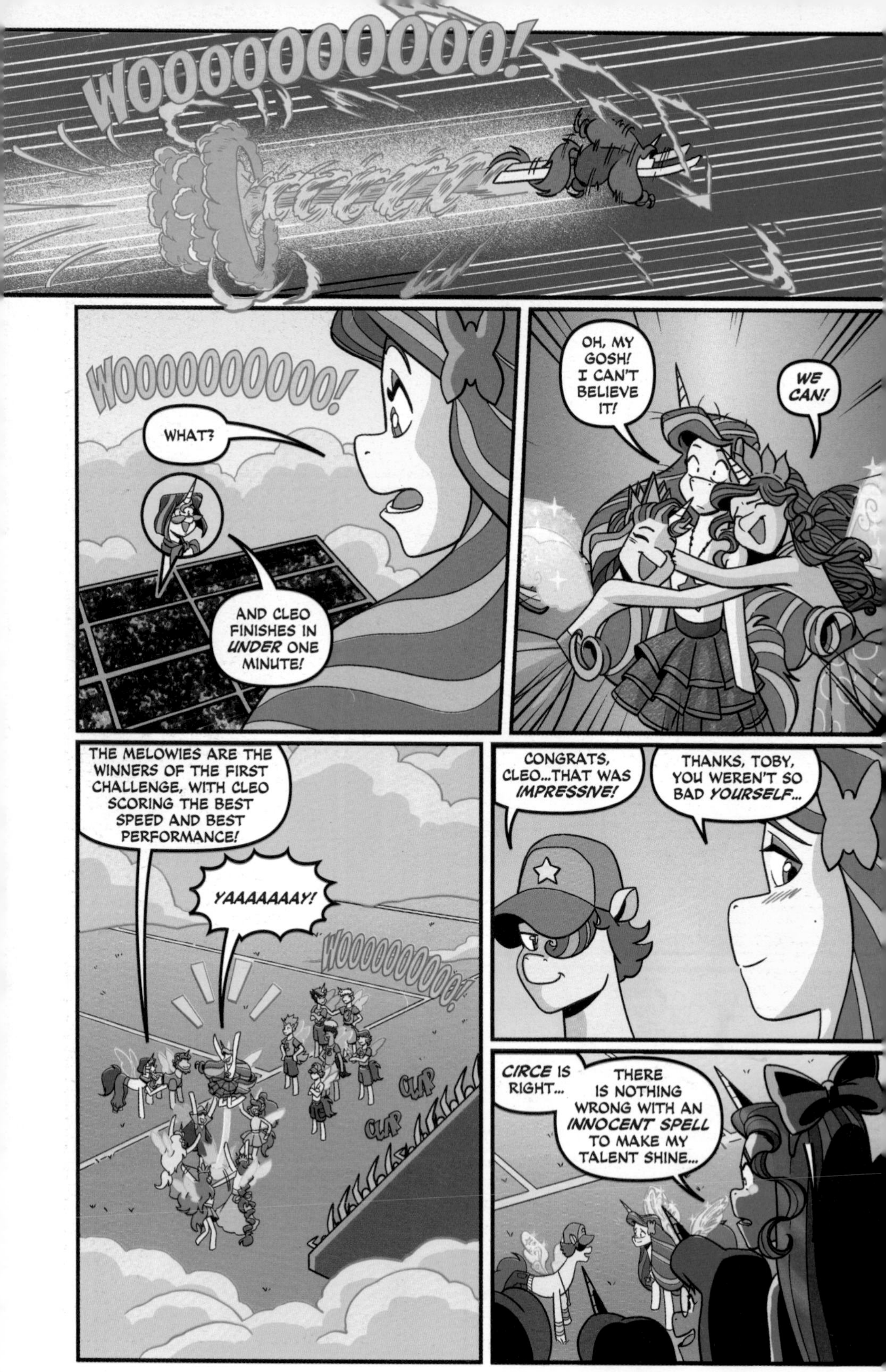
WOOOOOOOOOO!
WOOOOOOOOOOO!
WHAT?
AND CLEO FINISHES IN *UNDER* ONE MINUTE!
OH, MY GOSH! I CAN'T BELIEVE IT!
WE CAN!
THE MELOWIES ARE THE WINNERS OF THE FIRST CHALLENGE, WITH CLEO SCORING THE BEST SPEED AND BEST PERFORMANCE!
YAAAAAAAY!
WOOOOOOOOOOO!
CLAP
CLAP
CONGRATS, CLEO...THAT WAS *IMPRESSIVE!*
THANKS, TOBY, YOU WEREN'T SO BAD *YOURSELF*...
CIRCE IS RIGHT...
THERE IS NOTHING WRONG WITH AN *INNOCENT SPELL* TO MAKE MY TALENT SHINE...

...BY BORROWING SOME OF *CLEO'S*...

...ALL I HAVE TO DO IS PLACE CLEO'S STRAND OF HAIR INSIDE THIS MAGICAL *PENDANT*...

...AND HER *TALENTS* WILL TRANSFER OVER TO ME...

...AFTER ALL, IT'LL TEACH HER TO BE MORE HUMBLE, LIKE *CIRCE* SAID.

A BIT LATER, IN DESTINY'S GARDEN, TOBY IS TEACHING CLEO SOME TRICKS ON HIS *LIGHT BOARD!*

FIRST OF ALL, LET GO OF YOUR *FEAR* AND *RELAX!*

HOW? IT'S SO *UNSTEADY!*

DEEP BREATHS...FIND YOUR BALANCE, AND THINK OF THE LIGHT BOARD AS AN EXTENSION OF YOURSELF...

O--KAY...

HOW CAN A MELOWY LIKE *YOU* BE AFRAID OF A LIGHT BOARD?

WHAT DO YOU MEAN?

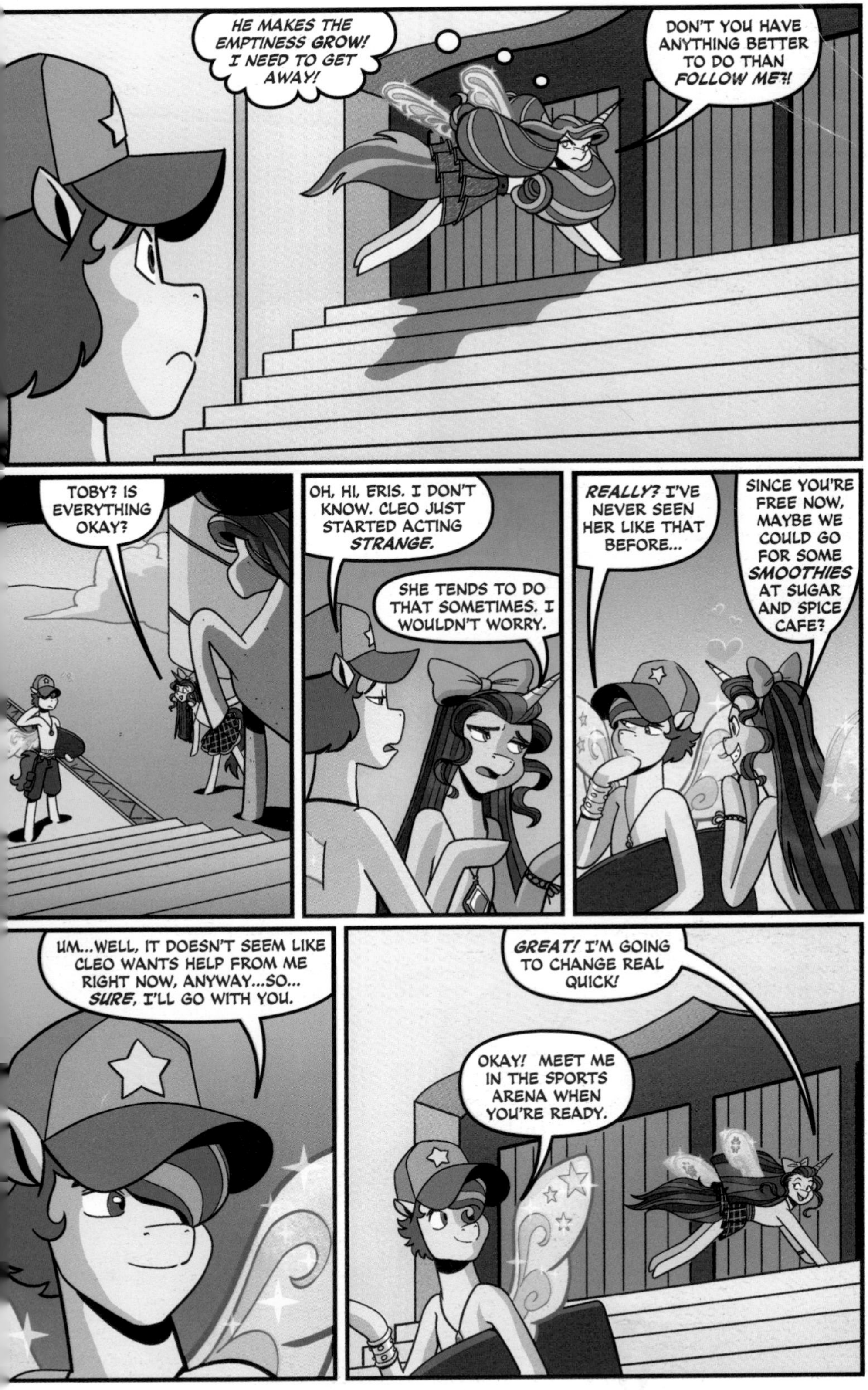
HE MAKES THE EMPTINESS GROW! I NEED TO GET AWAY!
DON'T YOU HAVE ANYTHING BETTER TO DO THAN FOLLOW ME?!
TOBY? IS EVERYTHING OKAY?
OH, HI, ERIS. I DON'T KNOW. CLEO JUST STARTED ACTING STRANGE.
SHE TENDS TO DO THAT SOMETIMES. I WOULDN'T WORRY.
REALLY? I'VE NEVER SEEN HER LIKE THAT BEFORE...
SINCE YOU'RE FREE NOW, MAYBE WE COULD GO FOR SOME SMOOTHIES AT SUGAR AND SPICE CAFE?
UM...WELL, IT DOESN'T SEEM LIKE CLEO WANTS HELP FROM ME RIGHT NOW, ANYWAY...SO... SURE, I'LL GO WITH YOU.
GREAT! I'M GOING TO CHANGE REAL QUICK!
OKAY! MEET ME IN THE SPORTS ARENA WHEN YOU'RE READY.

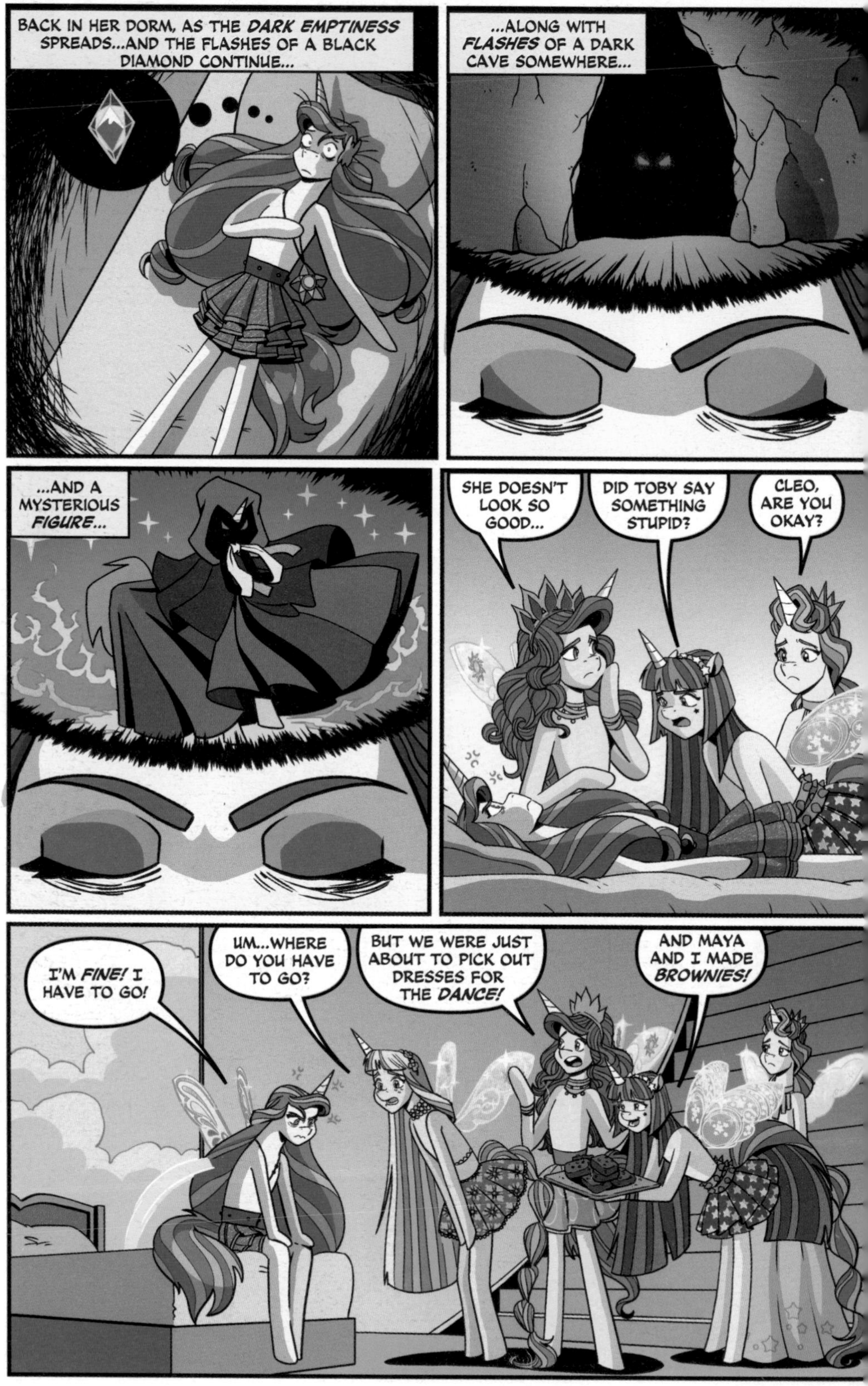
BACK IN HER DORM, AS THE *DARK EMPTINESS* SPREADS...AND THE FLASHES OF A BLACK DIAMOND CONTINUE...
...ALONG WITH *FLASHES* OF A DARK CAVE SOMEWHERE...
...AND A MYSTERIOUS *FIGURE*...
SHE DOESN'T LOOK SO GOOD...
DID TOBY SAY SOMETHING STUPID?
CLEO, ARE YOU OKAY?
I'M *FINE!* I HAVE TO GO!
UM...WHERE DO YOU HAVE TO GO?
BUT WE WERE JUST ABOUT TO PICK OUT DRESSES FOR THE *DANCE!*
AND MAYA AND I MADE *BROWNIES!*

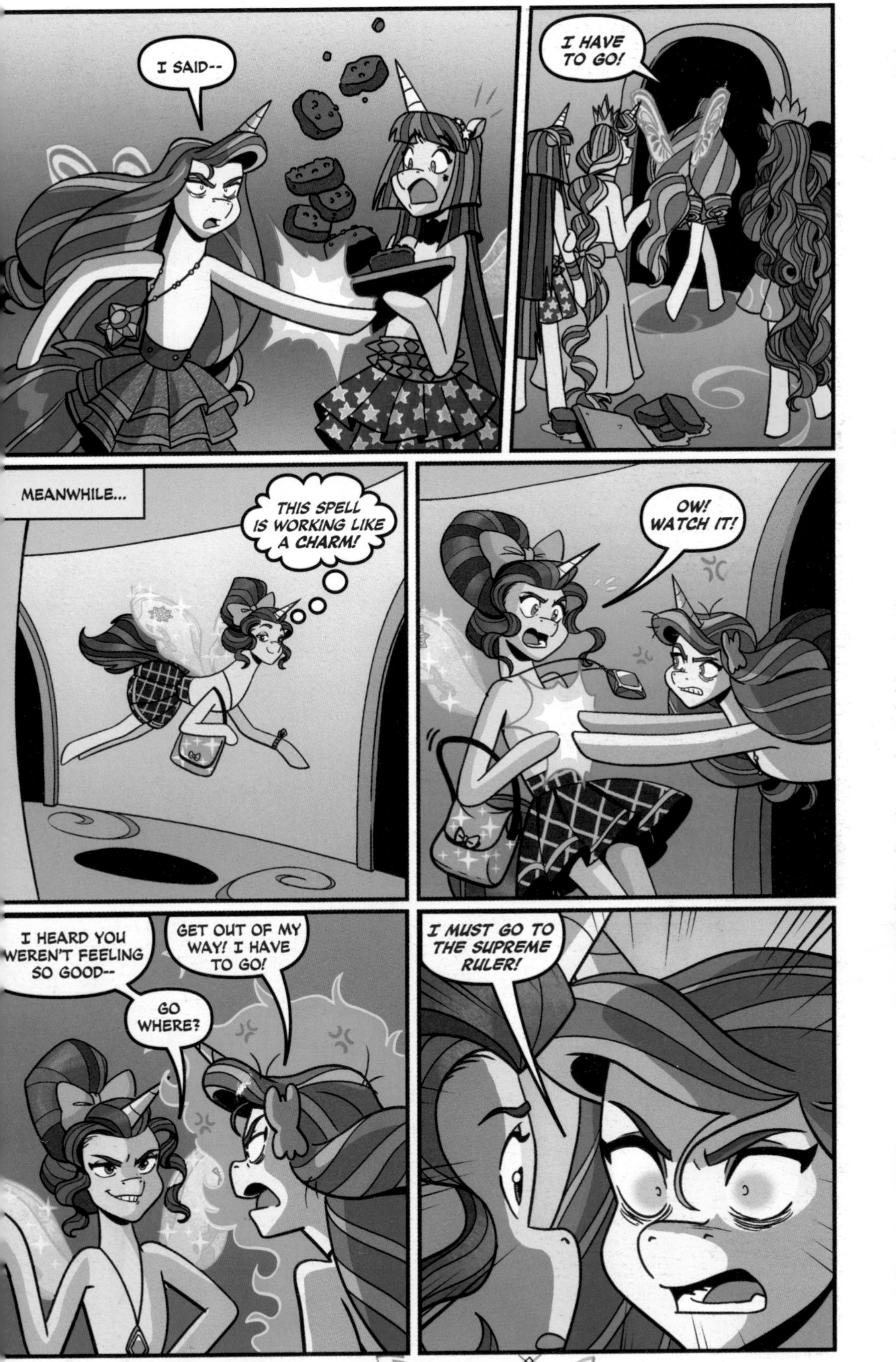
I SAID--
I HAVE TO GO!
MEANWHILE...
THIS SPELL IS WORKING LIKE A CHARM!
OW! WATCH IT!
I HEARD YOU WEREN'T FEELING SO GOOD--
GET OUT OF MY WAY! I HAVE TO GO!
GO WHERE?
I MUST GO TO THE SUPREME RULER!

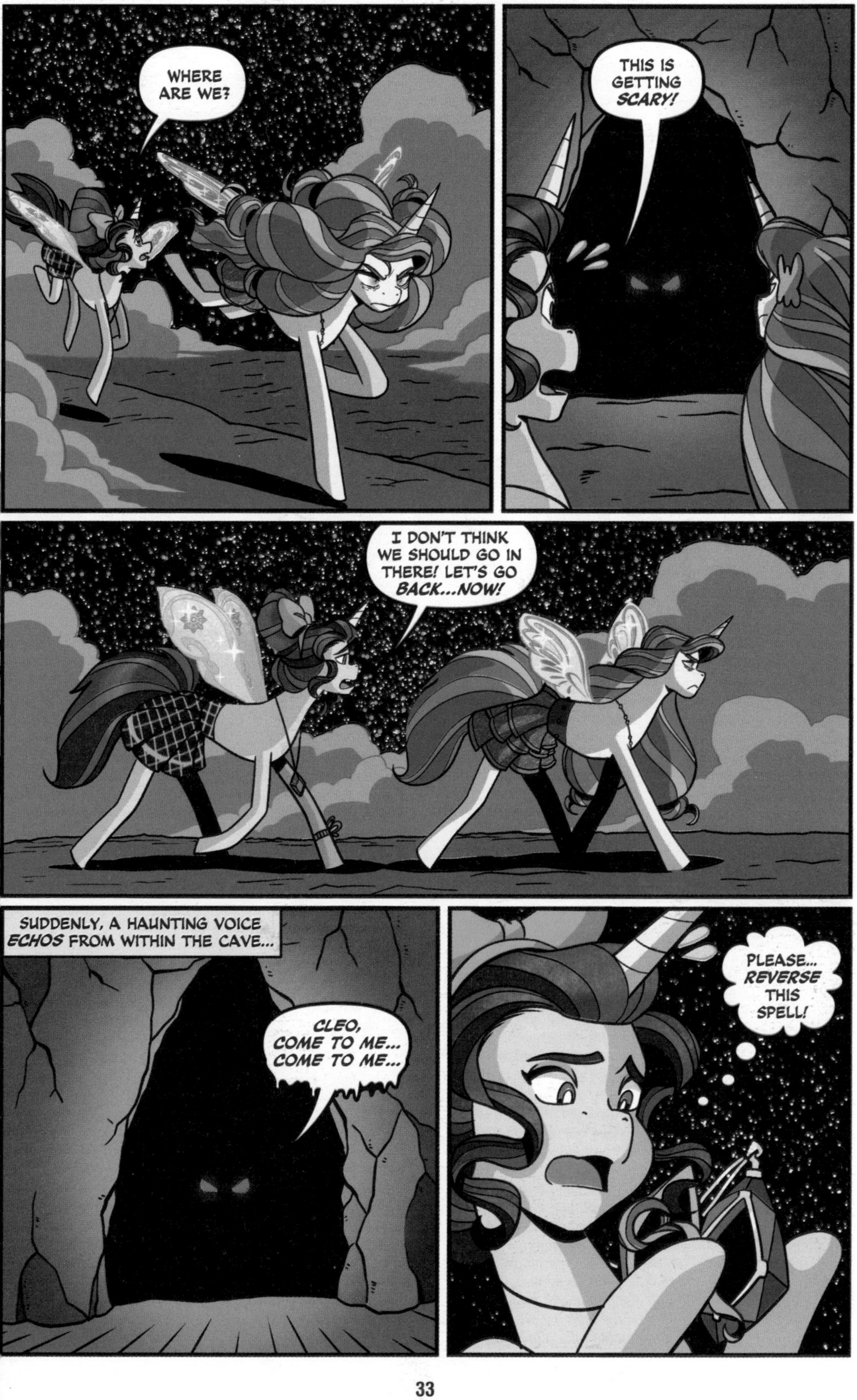
WHERE ARE WE?
THIS IS GETTING SCARY!
I DON'T THINK WE SHOULD GO IN THERE! LET'S GO BACK...NOW!
SUDDENLY, A HAUNTING VOICE ECHOS FROM WITHIN THE CAVE...
CLEO, COME TO ME... COME TO ME...
PLEASE... REVERSE THIS SPELL!

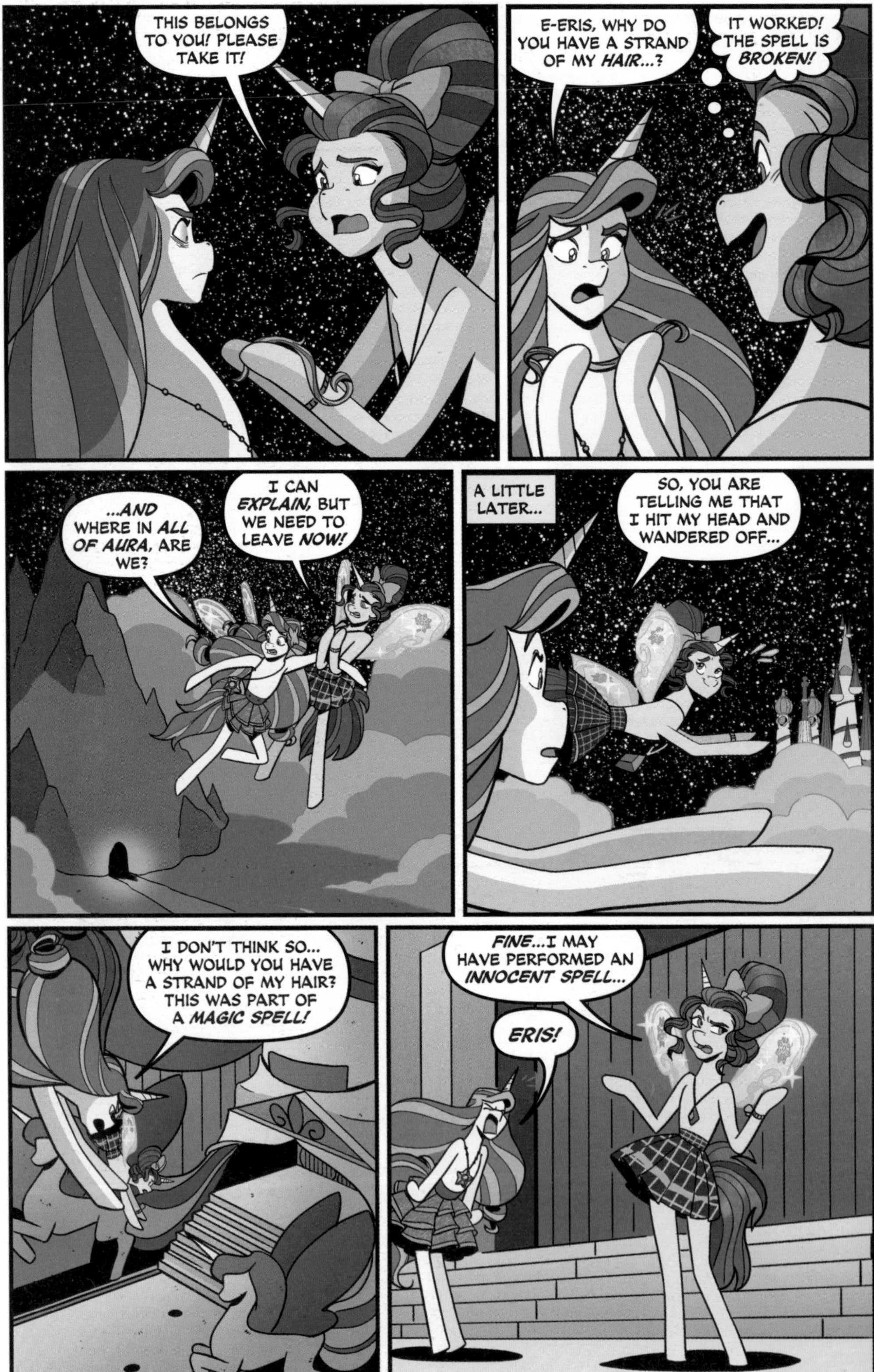
THIS BELONGS TO YOU! PLEASE TAKE IT!
E-ERIS, WHY DO YOU HAVE A STRAND OF MY HAIR...?
IT WORKED! THE SPELL IS BROKEN!
...AND WHERE IN ALL OF AURA, ARE WE?
I CAN EXPLAIN, BUT WE NEED TO LEAVE NOW!
A LITTLE LATER...
SO, YOU ARE TELLING ME THAT I HIT MY HEAD AND WANDERED OFF...
I DON'T THINK SO... WHY WOULD YOU HAVE A STRAND OF MY HAIR? THIS WAS PART OF A MAGIC SPELL!
FINE...I MAY HAVE PERFORMED AN INNOCENT SPELL...
ERIS!

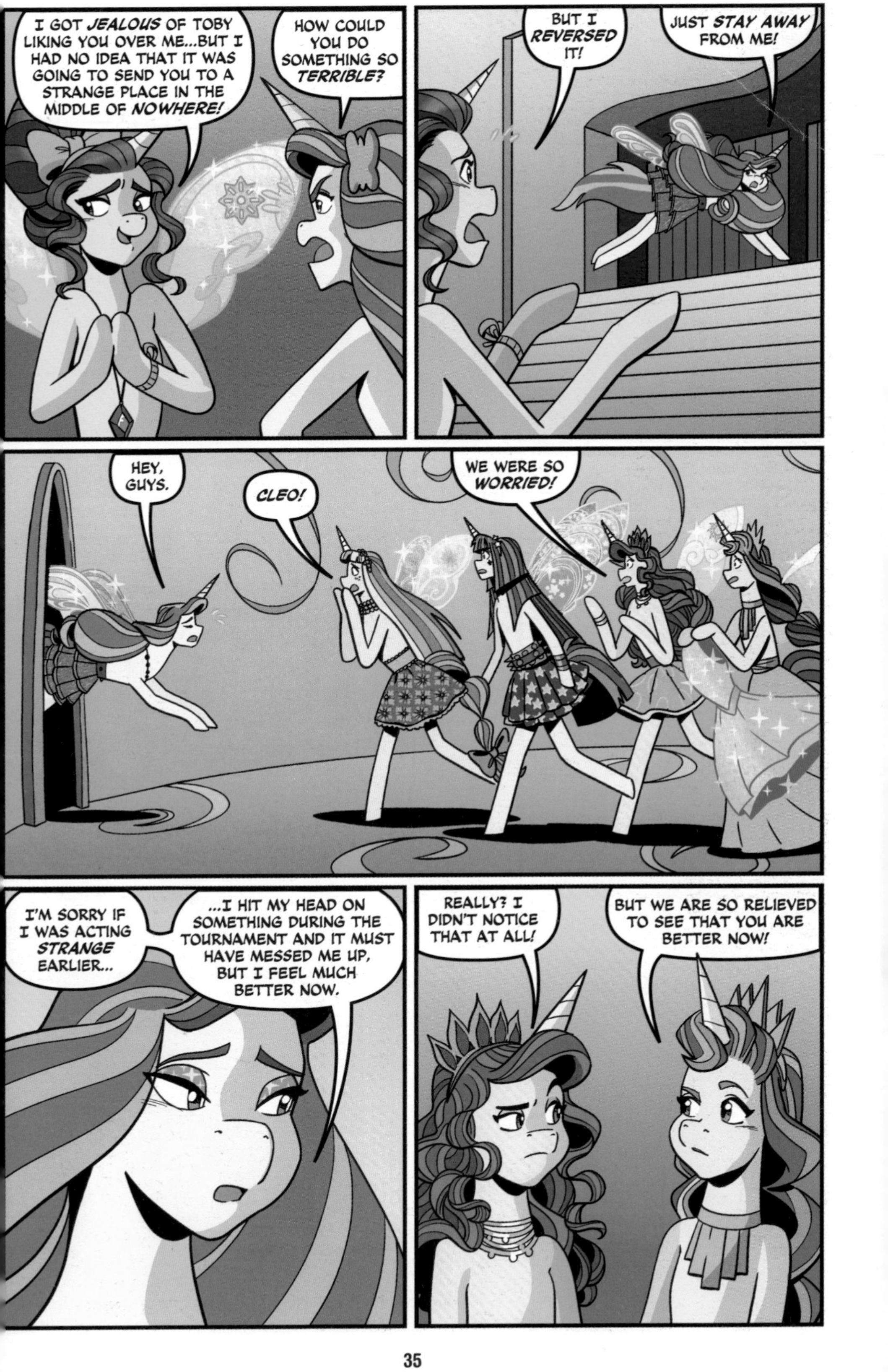
I GOT JEALOUS OF TOBY LIKING YOU OVER ME...BUT I HAD NO IDEA THAT IT WAS GOING TO SEND YOU TO A STRANGE PLACE IN THE MIDDLE OF NOWHERE!
HOW COULD YOU DO SOMETHING SO TERRIBLE?
BUT I REVERSED IT!
JUST STAY AWAY FROM ME!
HEY, GUYS.
CLEO!
WE WERE SO WORRIED!
I'M SORRY IF I WAS ACTING STRANGE EARLIER...
...I HIT MY HEAD ON SOMETHING DURING THE TOURNAMENT AND IT MUST HAVE MESSED ME UP, BUT I FEEL MUCH BETTER NOW.
REALLY? I DIDN'T NOTICE THAT AT ALL!
BUT WE ARE SO RELIEVED TO SEE THAT YOU ARE BETTER NOW!

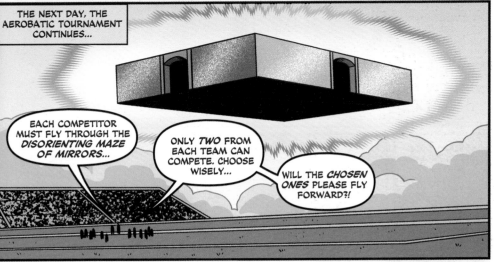

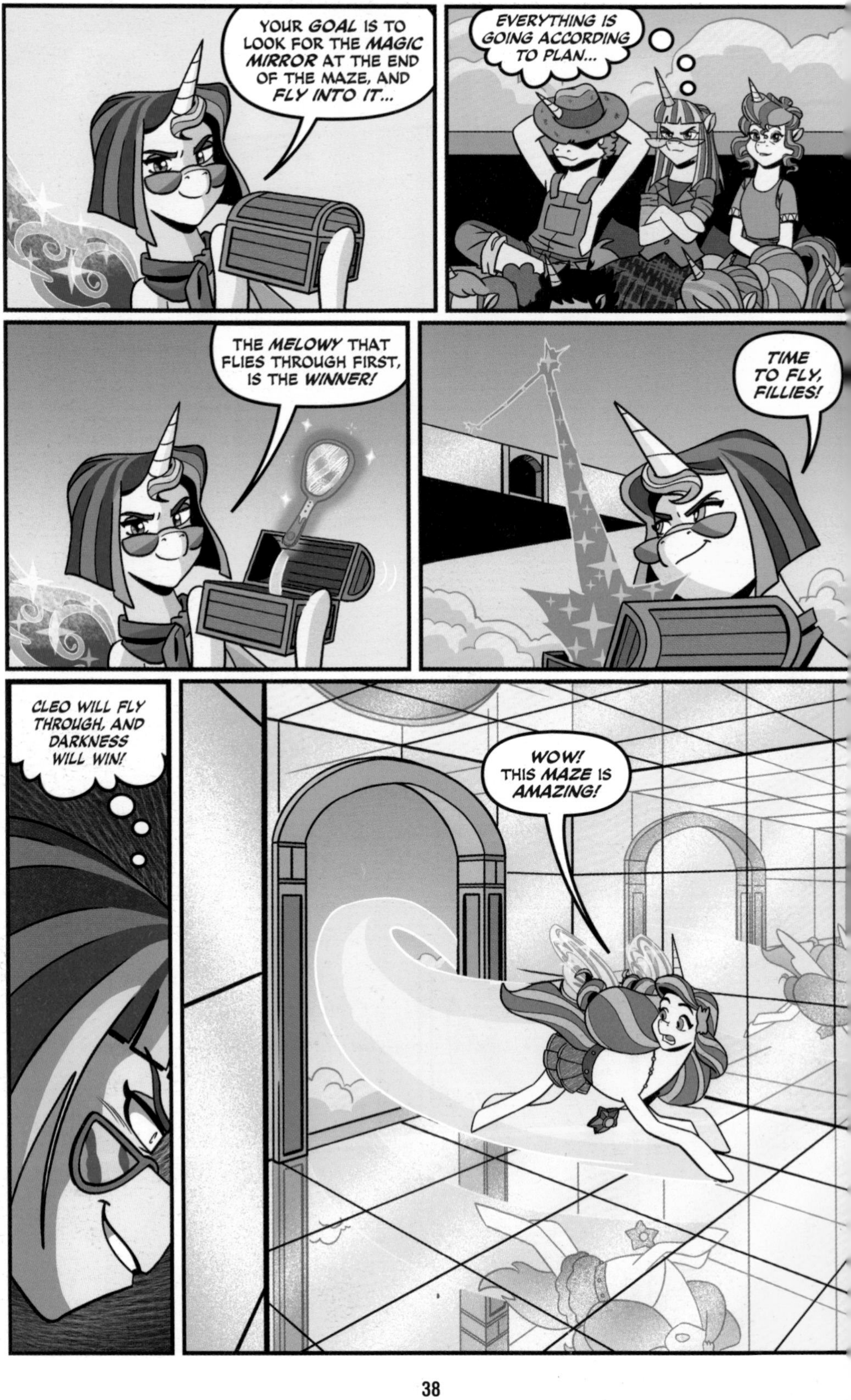
YOUR GOAL IS TO LOOK FOR THE MAGIC MIRROR AT THE END OF THE MAZE, AND FLY INTO IT...
EVERYTHING IS GOING ACCORDING TO PLAN...
THE MELOWY THAT FLIES THROUGH FIRST, IS THE WINNER!
TIME TO FLY, FILLIES!
CLEO WILL FLY THROUGH, AND DARKNESS WILL WIN!
WOW! THIS MAZE IS AMAZING!

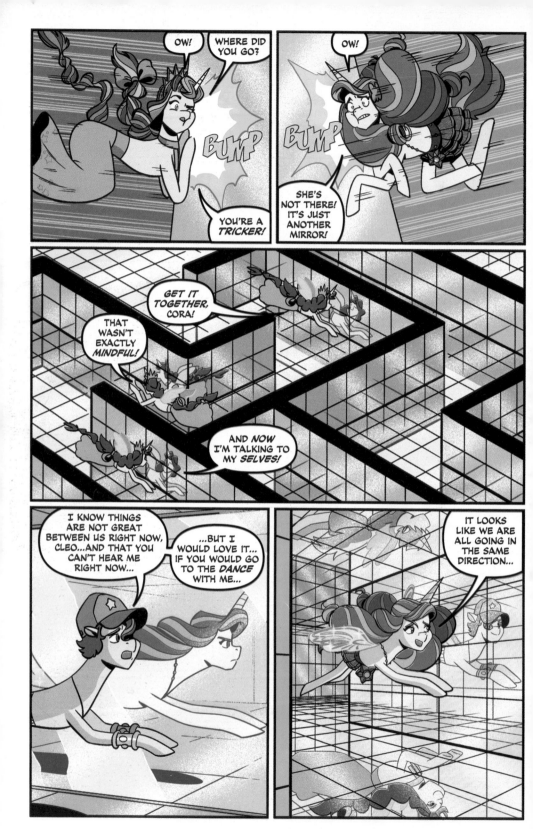

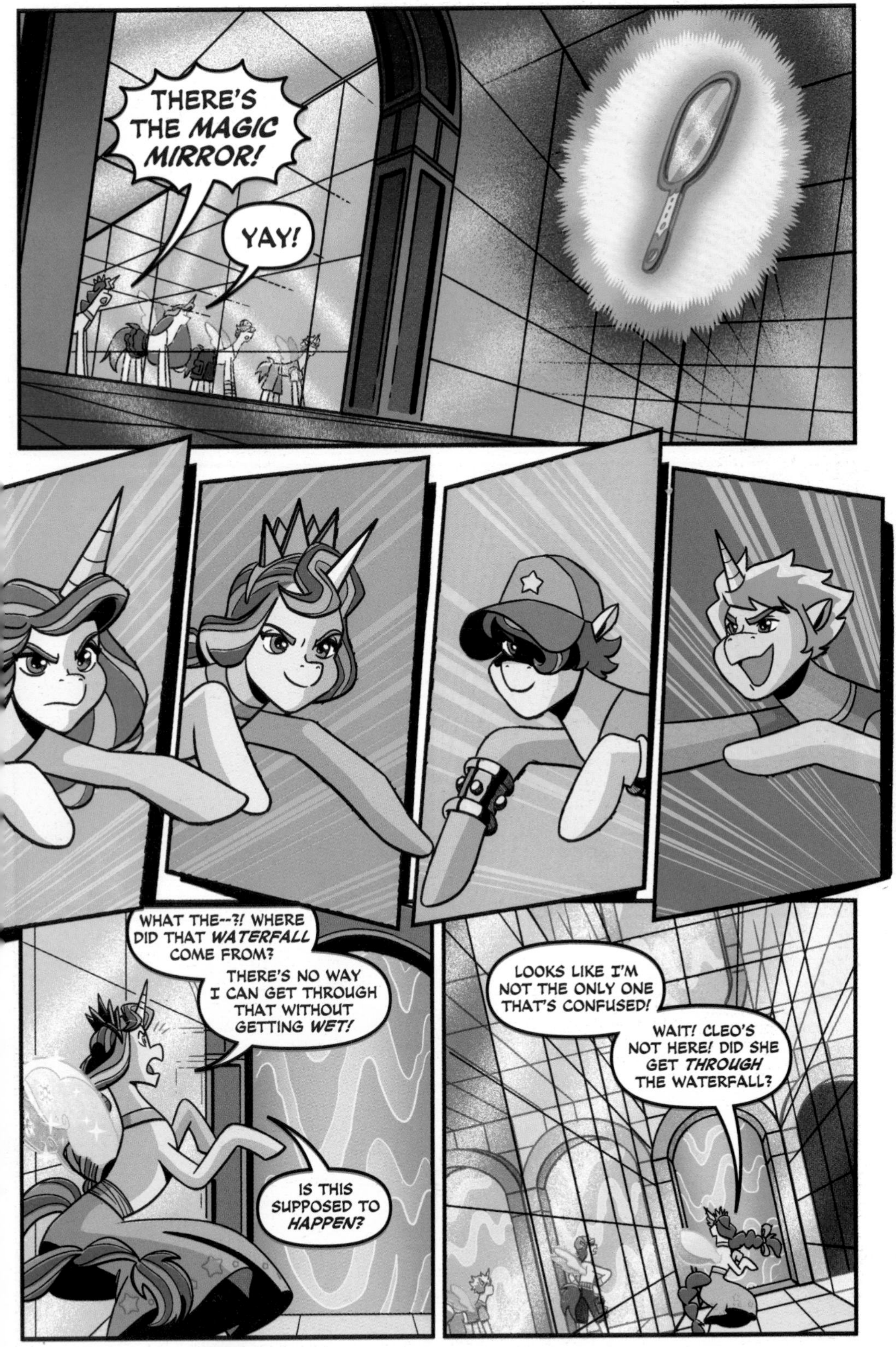
THERE'S THE *MAGIC MIRROR!*
YAY!
WHAT THE--?! WHERE DID THAT *WATERFALL* COME FROM?
THERE'S NO WAY I CAN GET THROUGH THAT WITHOUT GETTING *WET!*
IS THIS SUPPOSED TO *HAPPEN?*
LOOKS LIKE I'M NOT THE ONLY ONE THAT'S CONFUSED!
WAIT! CLEO'S NOT HERE! DID SHE GET *THROUGH* THE WATERFALL?

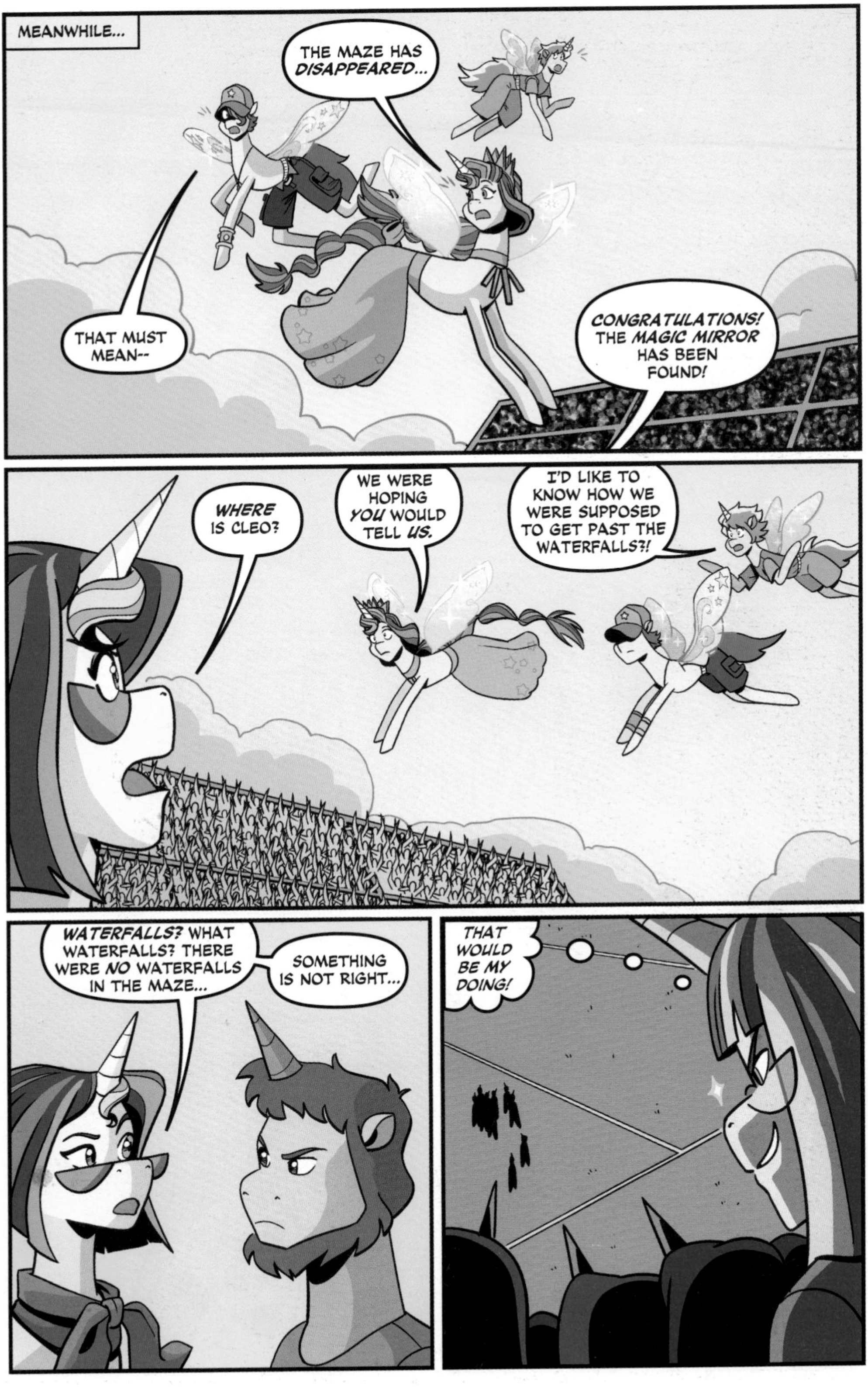
MEANWHILE...
THE MAZE HAS DISAPPEARED...
THAT MUST MEAN--
CONGRATULATIONS! THE MAGIC MIRROR HAS BEEN FOUND!
WHERE IS CLEO?
WE WERE HOPING YOU WOULD TELL US.
I'D LIKE TO KNOW HOW WE WERE SUPPOSED TO GET PAST THE WATERFALLS?!
WATERFALLS? WHAT WATERFALLS? THERE WERE NO WATERFALLS IN THE MAZE...
SOMETHING IS NOT RIGHT...
THAT WOULD BE MY DOING!

47

STILL THINK YOU DISARMED ME, GIA?! *I HAVE THE STAR!*

CLEO! I'M SO GLAD YOU'RE OKAY!

THIS PLACE IS NOT SAFE! WE ALL NEED TO LEAVE BEFORE THE *CAVE COLLAPSES!*

NOT YET...THAT *EVIL* PEGASUS, HAS MY STAR NECKLACE!

THERE IS ONE DETAIL YOU ARE MISSING...

NO! STOP! *STOP!*

THE STAR SERVES *ONE* PURPOSE...

NO! IT'S *MINE!* COME BACK!

49

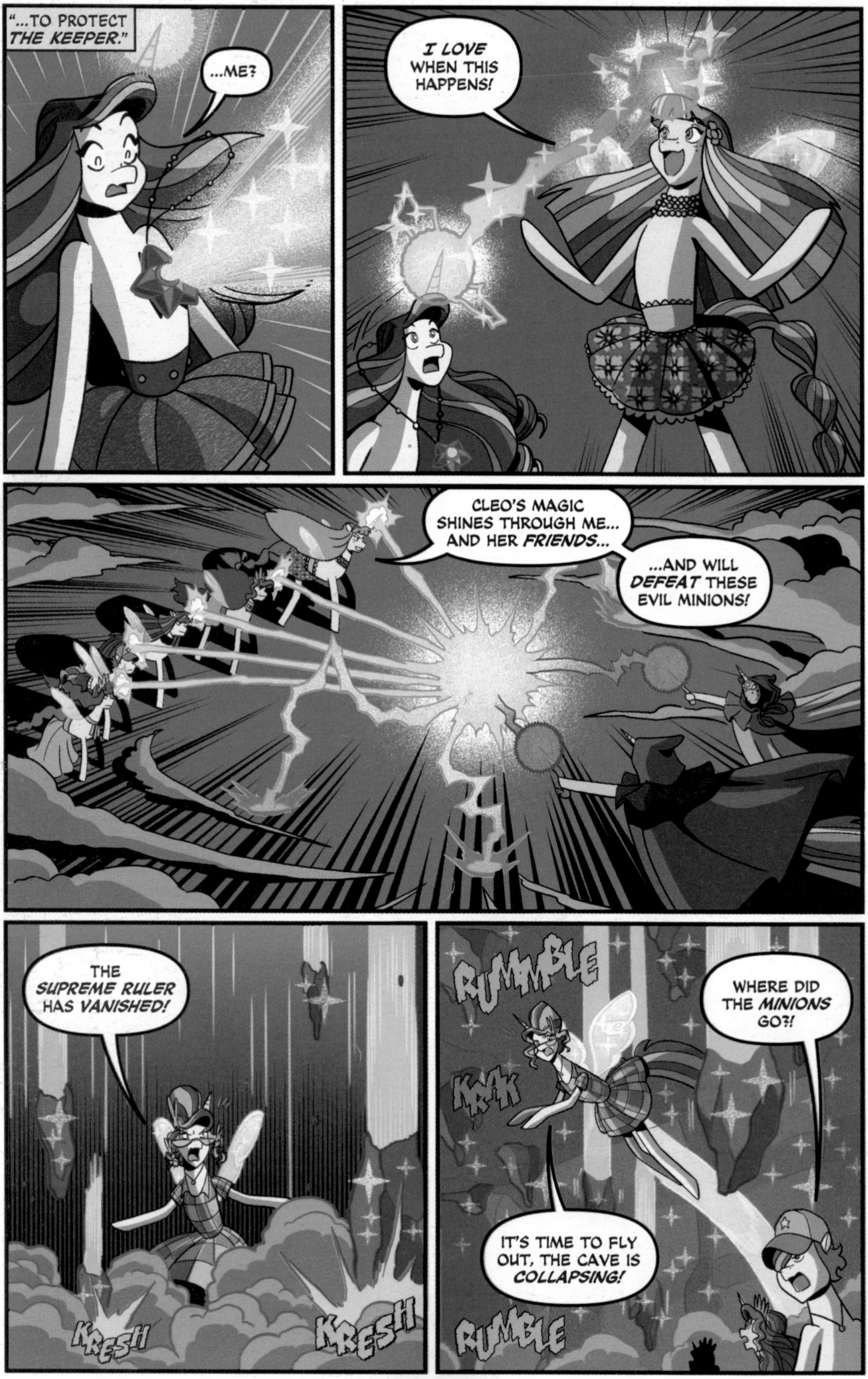
"...TO PROTECT THE KEEPER."
...ME?
I LOVE WHEN THIS HAPPENS!
CLEO'S MAGIC SHINES THROUGH ME... AND HER FRIENDS...
...AND WILL DEFEAT THESE EVIL MINIONS!
THE SUPREME RULER HAS VANISHED!
KRESH
KRESH
RUMMBLE
KRAK
WHERE DID THE MINIONS GO?!
IT'S TIME TO FLY OUT, THE CAVE IS COLLAPSING!
RUMBLE

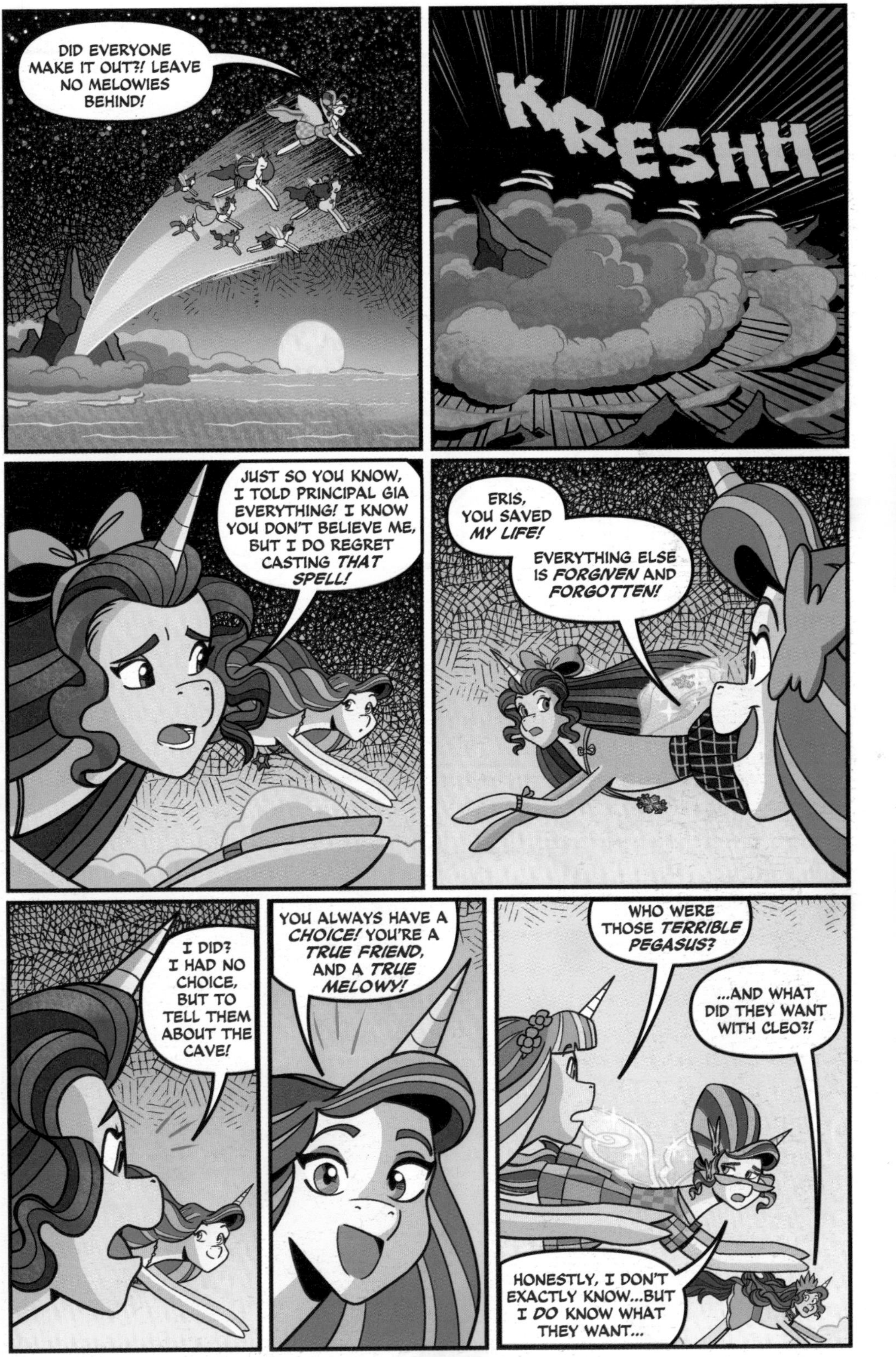
DID EVERYONE MAKE IT OUT?! LEAVE NO MELOWIES BEHIND!
KRESHH
JUST SO YOU KNOW, I TOLD PRINCIPAL GIA EVERYTHING! I KNOW YOU DON'T BELIEVE ME, BUT I DO REGRET CASTING THAT SPELL!
ERIS, YOU SAVED MY LIFE!
EVERYTHING ELSE IS FORGIVEN AND FORGOTTEN!
I DID? I HAD NO CHOICE, BUT TO TELL THEM ABOUT THE CAVE!
YOU ALWAYS HAVE A CHOICE! YOU'RE A TRUE FRIEND, AND A TRUE MELOWY!
WHO WERE THOSE TERRIBLE PEGASUS?
...AND WHAT DID THEY WANT WITH CLEO?!
HONESTLY, I DON'T EXACTLY KNOW...BUT I DO KNOW WHAT THEY WANT...

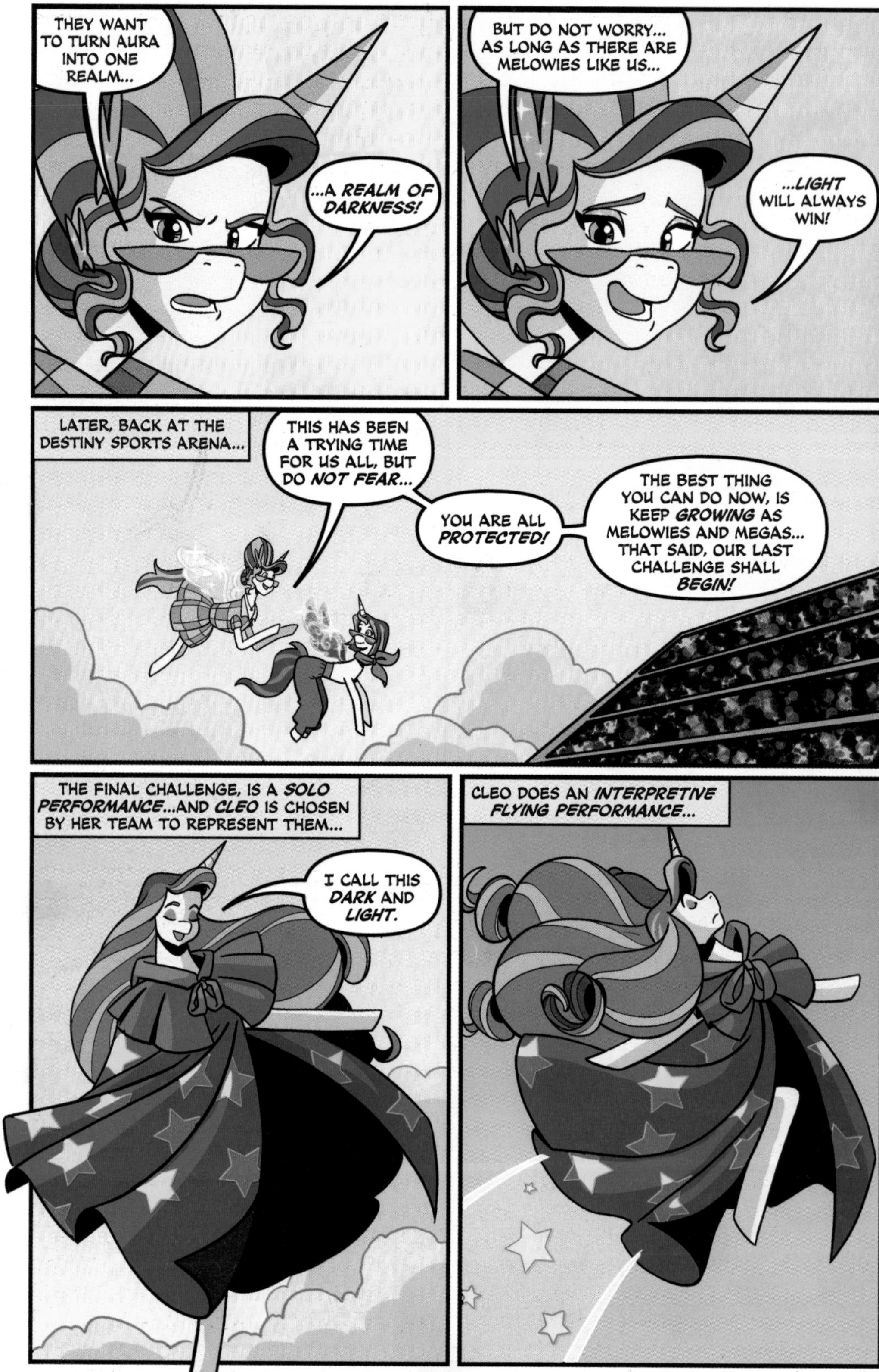
THEY WANT TO TURN AURA INTO ONE REALM...
...A *REALM OF DARKNESS!*
BUT DO NOT WORRY... AS LONG AS THERE ARE MELOWIES LIKE US...
...*LIGHT* WILL ALWAYS WIN!
LATER, BACK AT THE DESTINY SPORTS ARENA...
THIS HAS BEEN A TRYING TIME FOR US ALL, BUT DO *NOT FEAR...*
YOU ARE ALL *PROTECTED!*
THE BEST THING YOU CAN DO NOW, IS KEEP *GROWING* AS MELOWIES AND MEGAS... THAT SAID, OUR LAST CHALLENGE SHALL *BEGIN!*
THE FINAL CHALLENGE, IS A *SOLO PERFORMANCE*...AND *CLEO* IS CHOSEN BY HER TEAM TO REPRESENT THEM...
I CALL THIS *DARK* AND *LIGHT*.
CLEO DOES AN *INTERPRETIVE FLYING PERFORMANCE*...

...AND SHE BEGINS WITH THE *DANCE OF DARKNESS!*

...DEMONSTRATING THE *LONELINESS* INSIDE A *DARK MIND*...

...AS THE CLOAK FALLS TO THE GROUND, SHE FLIES HIGH INTO THE SKY...

...DEMONSTRATING THAT *LETTING GO* OF DARKNESS WILL REVEAL THE *LIGHT.*

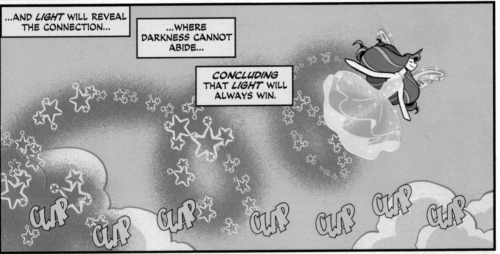

...AND *LIGHT* WILL REVEAL THE CONNECTION...

...WHERE DARKNESS CANNOT ABIDE...

CONCLUDING THAT *LIGHT* WILL ALWAYS WIN.

CLAP CLAP CLAP CLAP CLAP CLAP CLAP

THE MELOWIES *WON* WITH FLYING COLORS...

AND THE *CELEBRATORY DANCE* STARTS *NOW!*

END

WATCH OUT FOR PAPERCUTZ™

Welcome to the timely, talent-testing, third MELOWY graphic novel by "Coach" Cortney Powell and Ryan "Judge" Jampole based on the competitive characters created by "Drill Instructor" Danielle (All) Star, gamely brought to you by Papercutz, those winning folks dedicated to publishing great graphic novels for all ages. I'm Jim Salicrup, the Editor-in-Chief and the Destiny Aerobatic Team mascot, here to talk about all things MELOWY and Papercutz...

Seeing the Aerobatic Tournament featured in this MELOWY graphic novel reminded us of the Olympics, which reminds us of another wonderful Papercutz graphic novel, GERONIMO STILTON #10 "Geronimo Stilton Saves the Olympics." As you know, Geronimo is the editor-in-chief of Mouse Island's *Rodent's Gazette*, and quite often finds himself travelling back in time to save the future, by protecting the past — usually from those pesky Pirate Cats. Believe it or not, the Pirate Cats thought they could change history by winning the first Olympics back in 1894, but Geronimo was not about to let that happen. He went so far as to actually compete in that premiere Olympics himself!

And how could I forget about another Papercutz graphic novel, THE SMURFS #11 "The Smurf Olympics," where we got to see our little blue buddies compete in lots of Olympic events? Turns out those guys are incredibly competitive. In SMURFS THE VILLAGE BEHIND THE WALL #2 "The Betrayal of Smurfblossom," we see the female Smurfs (introduced in the movie *Smurfs: The Lost Village*) compete in the Great Smurf Tree Games. Things get really interesting when the Smurfy Grove champion is challenged by Handy Smurf. Perhaps the most unexpected competition of all takes place in THE SMURFS #25 "The Gambling Smurfs," when the Smurfs Village is threatened to be destroyed to make room for a casino, and Papa Smurf enlists Gargamel to represent the Smurfs in a tournament against these scoundrels. The results are surprising and hilarious.

Even if you're not a Melowy, a Smurf, or even a mouse, it's easy to get caught up with the competitive side of life. Whether it's being involved in sports, pageants, playing video games, getting good grades, or whatever challenges you may face, the thing to always remember is to simply try to be the best you that you can be. Follow your own interests. Just like the Melowies, you can attend school and discover what your true power is. One of the little things I enjoyed about "Time to Fly" was how supportive Cleo's friends were of her, well, all of them except Eris. Instead of being jealous of her success, they were happy for her. Competition can be healthy, and bring the best out of us, or in some cases it could bring out the worst (Looking at you, Eris!).

Speaking of competition, do you realize how many people and companies are competing just for your attention? Bet you didn't realize how important you are! Every day you're bombarded with commercials trying to get you to see certain TV shows or movies, eat breakfast cereals or Happy Meals, play with specific dolls or video games. Even when you go to a bookstore or library, hundreds of books are trying to get your attention so that you'll read them. At Papercutz we're also competing to get your attention — we do it by publishing the best graphic novels we possibly can. Here's an example of how competition focuses us on making sure we do our very best, to be worthy of your attention. We also do things such as attend Book Shows to get the word out about Papercutz graphic novels. Cortney Powell and Ryan Jampole were at a recent Brooklyn Book Festival in New York City, and loved meeting all the MELOWY fans who came by the Papercutz booth. And we want you to know we're very thankful that you're spending some of your valuable time with us.

Cortney "Coach" Powell   Ryan "Judge" Jampole

And what better way to conclude this mini-essay on competition, than by previewing THE SMURFS #25 "The Gambling Smurfs" and GERONIMO STILTON REPORTER #2 "It's My Scoop!," about the competition between Geronimo's newspaper and its rival, *The Daily Rat*. Seems like someone's been stealing Geronimo's scoops! See what we're talking about on the following pages.

Oh, we know we promised to include bios of MELOWY colorist Laurie E. Smith and letterer Wilson Ramos Jr. in this Watch Out for Papercutz column, but we had to reschedule it for MELOWY #4 "Frozen in Time," which is coming to your favorite bookseller or library soon. And there's even more we'd like to tell you about, but we're afraid it's time to fly!

Thanks,

STAY IN TOUCH!

EMAIL: salicrup@papercutz.com
WEB: papercutz.com
TWITTER: @papercutzgn
INSTAGRAM: @papercutzgn
FACEBOOK: PAPERCUTZGRAPHICNOVELS
FANMAIL: Papercutz, 160 Broadway, Suite 700, East Wing, New York, NY 10038

Here's a special preview of GERONIMO STILTON REPORTER #2 "It's My Scoop!"

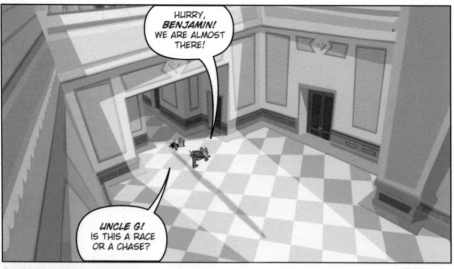

HURRY, *BENJAMIN!* WE ARE ALMOST THERE!

UNCLE G! IS THIS A RACE OR A CHASE?

NEITHER! THE NEW MAYOR'S PROMISED ME AN *EXCLUSIVE INTERVIEW* ON THE *CITY'S CENTENNIAL CELEBRATION!*

THE DAILY RAT'S BEEN BEATING ME TO ALL THE BIG STORIES LATELY...

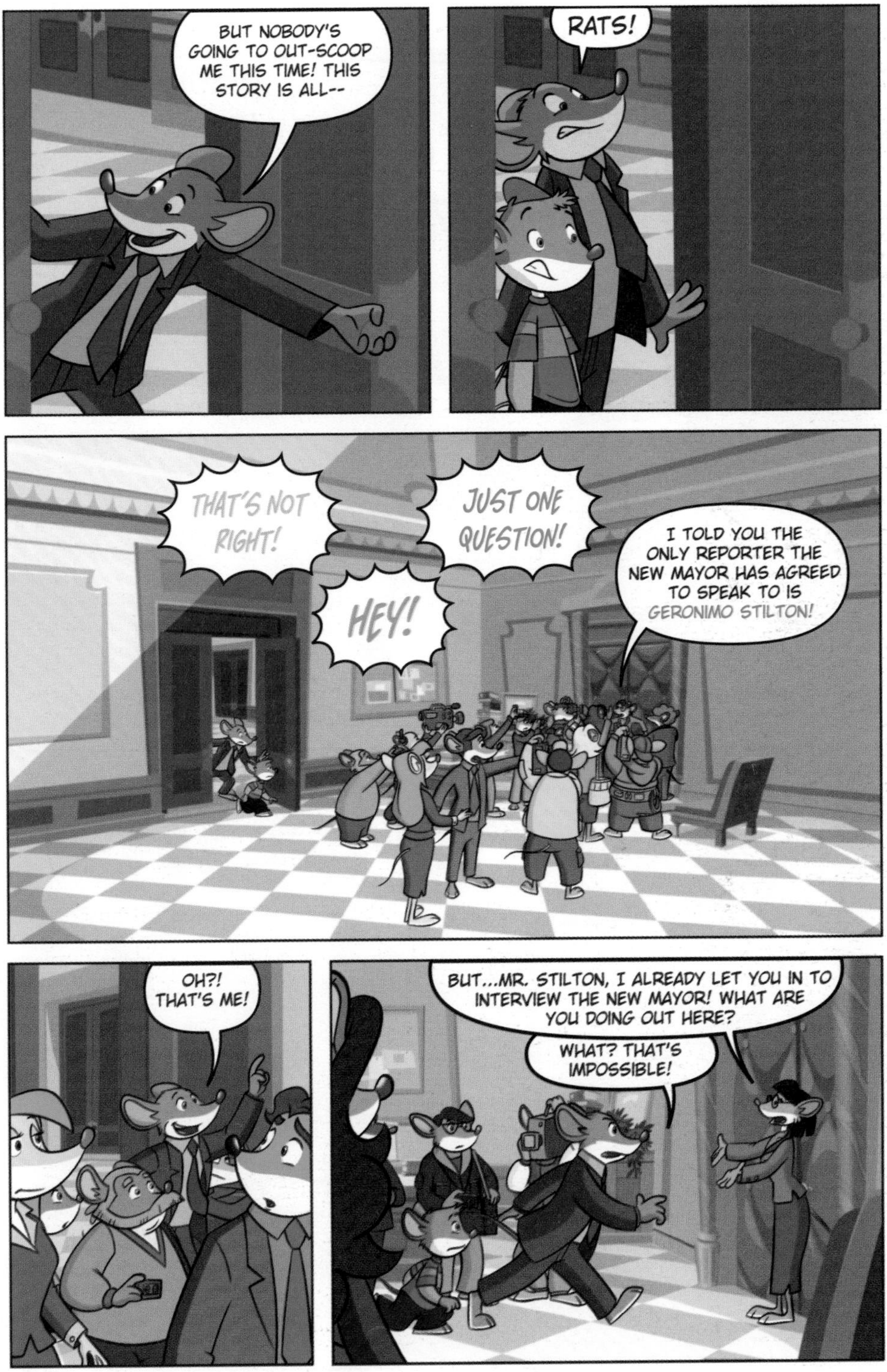
BUT NOBODY'S GOING TO OUT-SCOOP ME THIS TIME! THIS STORY IS ALL--
RATS!
THAT'S NOT RIGHT!
JUST ONE QUESTION!
HEY!
I TOLD YOU THE ONLY REPORTER THE NEW MAYOR HAS AGREED TO SPEAK TO IS GERONIMO STILTON!
OH?! THAT'S ME!
BUT...MR. STILTON, I ALREADY LET YOU IN TO INTERVIEW THE NEW MAYOR! WHAT ARE YOU DOING OUT HERE?
WHAT? THAT'S IMPOSSIBLE!

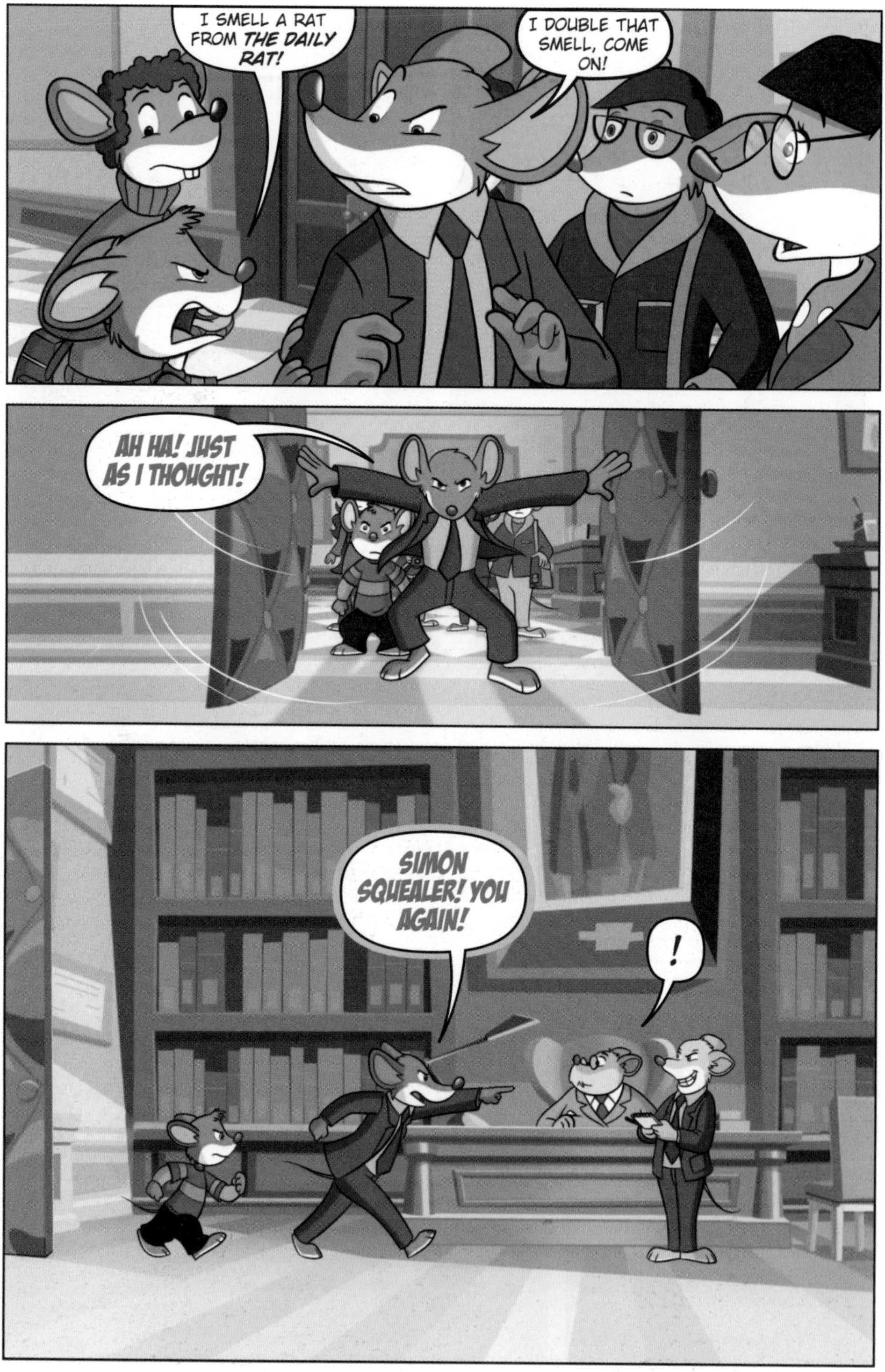
I SMELL A RAT FROM *THE DAILY RAT!*
I DOUBLE THAT SMELL, COME ON!
AH HA! JUST AS I THOUGHT!
SIMON SQUEALER! YOU AGAIN!
!

I CAN'T BELIEVE IT!

I WAS SCOOPED BY SIMON SQUEALER POSING AS ME!

HOW'D HE KNOW THAT THE NEW MAYOR WAS GIVING YOU THE EXCLUSIVE?

I DON'T KNOW, BUT THIS IS EXACTLY THE KIND OF UNDERHANDED TACTIC I'D EXPECT FROM SIMON'S BOSS, *SALLY RATMOUSEN!*

BIP
BIP BIP

HEADS UP! NEWSFLASH ON MY *BEN PAD!*

BIP

Don't miss GERONIMO STILTON REPORTER #2 "It's My Scoop!" available at booksellers and libraries now.

Here's a special bonus preview of THE SMURFS #25 "The Gambling Smurfs"...

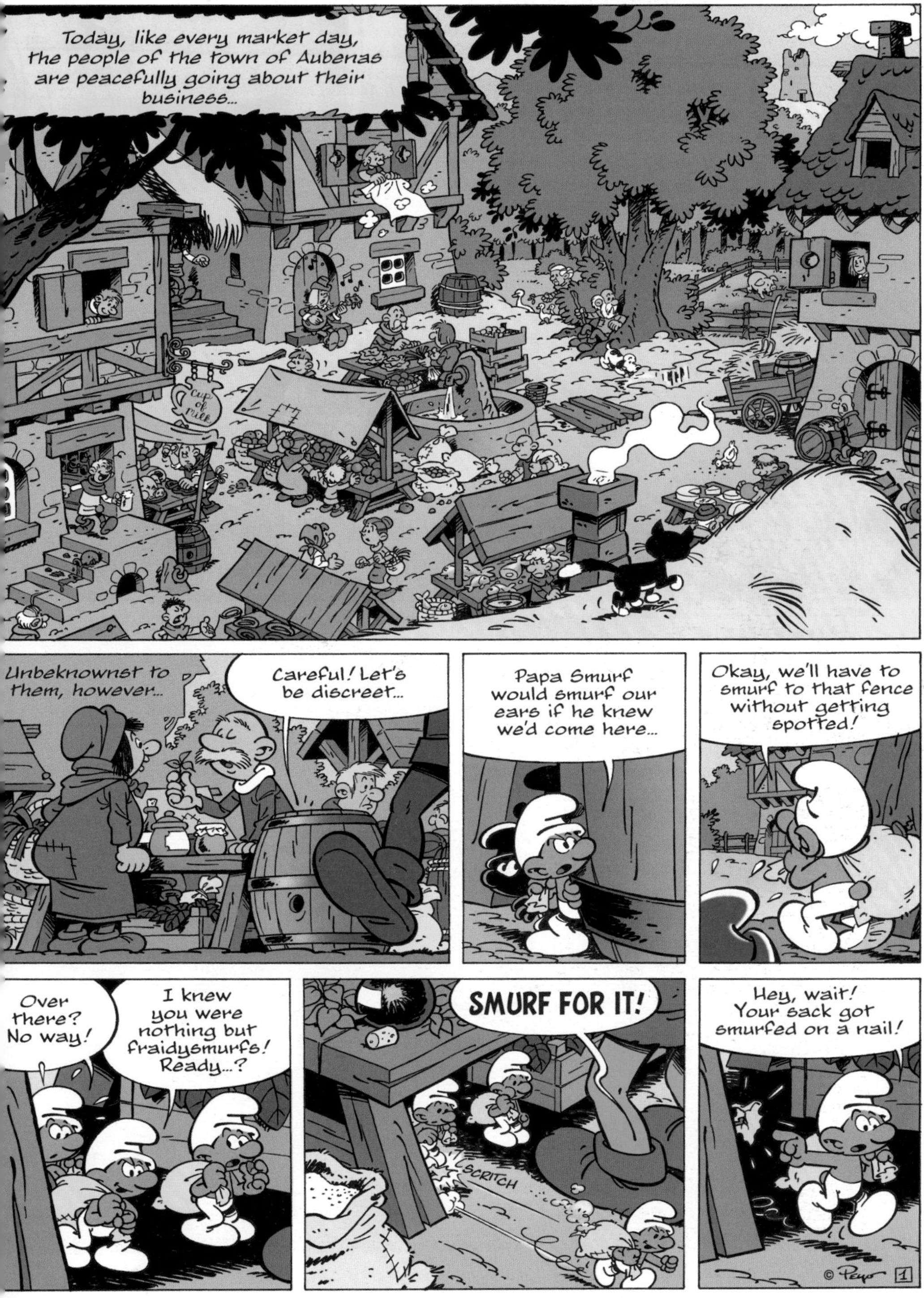
Today, like every market day, the people of the town of Aubenas are peacefully going about their business...
Cup of milk
Unbeknownst to them, however...
Careful! Let's be discreet...
Papa Smurf would smurf our ears if he knew we'd come here...
Okay, we'll have to smurf to that fence without getting spotted!
Over there? No way!
I knew you were nothing but fraidysmurfs! Ready...?
SMURF FOR IT!
SCRITCH
Hey, wait! Your sack got smurfed on a nail!
© Peyo
1

Good try! Last one there's a smurf!

Ha! Ha! Ha! I'm always first when Hefty Smurf's not around!

>CHOKE!< >KOF!< >KOF! KOF!<

?

Oooo... I'm sure Chef Smurf won't want to smurf me an extra dessert now!

ATCHOO!

Can you smurf me a little from your sack?

No way! Otherwise I'm the one risking not smurfing a dessert!

KOF KOF

AHA! KNAVE! YOUR FINAL HOUR HAS COME!

? !?

?

CLANG

You have no chance!

!

© Peyo

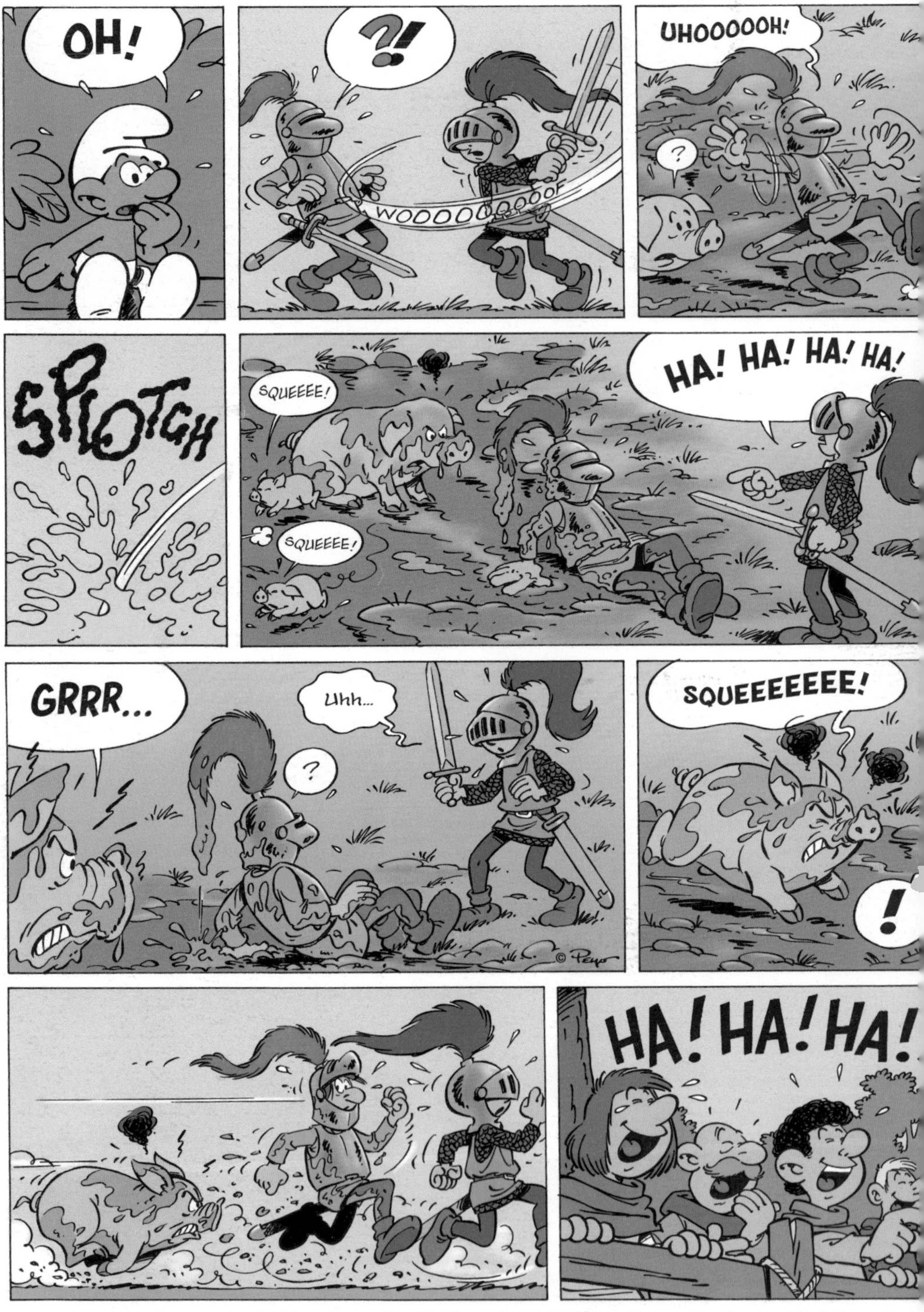
OH!
?!
WOOOOOOOOOOF
UHOOOOOH!
?
SPLOTCH
SQUEEEE!
SQUEEEE!
HA! HA! HA! HA!
GRRR...
Uhh...
?
© Peyo
SQUEEEEEEE!
!
HA! HA! HA!

Don't miss THE SMURFS #25 "The Gambling Smurfs," available at booksellers and libraries now.